To my ever-patient wife, Ruth.

Acknowledgements and thanks

In 2014, I prompted my daughter Heidi to write a Bible-based story. Her response was that I should show her how! This is my attempt to do so.

Particular thanks go to Ruth, my wife, who helped me find time to write, patiently read what I wrote, and humoured me when I spent inordinate amounts of time on research into minute details.

Feedback from early readers and subscribers has improved the story greatly, so I thank them. No manuscript is ever without errors, but these early readers helped eliminate most typos, bad grammar and uncomfortable usage. Cathy, my oldest daughter has tirelessly undertaken the thankless task of proof reading the entire manuscript more than once. Thanks, Cathy.

My son Chris has also helped with various technical details and his excellent reading has made the audio book a pleasure to listen to. I never expected to enjoy listening to anything I had written, but Chris achieved this.

A request

I have a request to make of all readers: if you find any errors; typos, spelling errors, poor grammar, unkempt use of vocabulary, or, most importantly, errors of fact where the story misrepresents the Bible, please let me know. I can't correct printed books, but electronic versions and any new printed editions can be fixed.

Terror on Every Side!

THE LIFE OF JEREMIAH

VOLUME 2 – As Good As It Gets

Mark Morgan

ISBN (eBook): 978-1-925587-11-1
ISBN (Paperback): 978-1-925587-01-2

Bible
Tales
www.BibleTales.online

Cover picture: Jerusalem from the Mount of Olives
by Frederick Edwin Church (1870).

Free Download

Paul in Snippets

A 109-page PDF novelette by Mark Morgan.

The life of Paul painted from the Acts of the Apostles.

Get your free copy of *Paul in Snippets* when you sign up for the Bible Tales mailing list. As well as the eBook, you will receive a weekly email newsletter with micro tales, informative articles and special offers.

Visit **http://www.BibleTales.online/free-pins**

Bible
Tales

www.BibleTales.online

VOLUME TWO

As Good As It Gets

Contents

"Terror on Every Side!"

For I hear the whispering of many—
terror on every side!—
as they scheme together against me,
as they plot to take my life.

> A psalm of David: Psalm 31:13

For I hear many whispering.
Terror is on every side!
"Denounce him! Let us denounce him!"
say all my close friends,
watching for my fall.
"Perhaps he will be deceived;
then we can overcome him
and take our revenge on him."

> Jeremiah 20:10

Chapter 1

News from Israel

September, 622 BC – the 18th year of King Josiah

I was twenty-one years old when the letter arrived. It was the most exciting letter I ever received. Written in my father's untidy scrawl, it had obviously been sent in the joy of discovery and his happiness showed in every word.

The Book of the Law of God had been found!

Perhaps the scroll had been hidden in the temple by a devoted priest during the dark and dangerous days of King Manasseh, or maybe it had rested unseen from earlier times. Whatever secrecy may have veiled its original concealment, its discovery will become a thing of legend that can never be forgotten.

In fact, it could be the most important thing ever found in Israel – and my father himself found it. Here is how it happened.

Having pursued the worship of God tirelessly from the age of sixteen, Josiah has finally turned his attention to the temple of Yahweh. You see, in response to Josiah's dedication to Yahweh, more and more people had begun to make offerings and donations for the temple and for the Levites, and at some stage, the idea of refurbishing the temple had taken hold of the nation. The worn and damaged stones were to be replaced, the tarnished and corroded metalwork attended to and the rotting timbers renewed. Bags of money and other offerings were being left in pots and cups in many places around the temple. Josiah had directed that the gatekeepers should collect all the money and valuable gifts together and deliver them to his administrators for safekeeping until the work could be organised, but nobody knew quite what to do. Such an overflowing generosity for the work of the temple had not been seen in the lifetime of any of the priests or Levites. Everyone agreed that the money should be collected in a more organised way, but how?

Some of the old priests had heard stories of the events in the time of King Joash, more than 200 years before, when the temple was last refurbished in any significant way. At that time, a hole had been bored in the top of a wooden chest so that the offerings of worshippers could be easily dropped in[1]. As the priests described the wooden chest, my father suddenly remembered seeing such a chest in one of the crowded storerooms of the temple many years before, during a short-lived attempt to free up some extra space in the temple. Storerooms always fill up, and the side rooms of the temple were no exception.

My father took a torch and made his way with some Levites to the storeroom in which he had seen the chest. Opening the heavy wooden door, they could see, in the flickering light of the torch, items stacked from floor to ceiling. Packed tightly together, they barely left room to open the door. Obviously, there had initially been narrow

---

[1] 2 Kings 12:9-15

spaces between ordered stacks, but over time these too had filled up. It took quite a while to find the chest, hidden as it was several cubits away from the door against the left wall. Clearly, it was very strong, since it had a pile more than four cubits[2] high of unwanted (but much too useful to throw out!) articles sitting on top of it. During the process of discovery, the storeroom disgorged a steady stream of items, and by the time the chest had been safely retrieved, the corridor outside was littered with thousands of artefacts, most of which would not have been actually used in worship for more than a century.

Finally, the chest was dragged from the room and the process of re-stacking all of the displaced articles began.

My father, however, began to examine his newly discovered prize. On the top, the chest had a board across the back, and the lid had projections which hooked under this board so that it could not be removed if a single fastener was in place at the front of the chest. This fastener held down the front of the lid, and the projections hooked under the board at the rear so that less honest visitors could not easily help themselves to the contents of the chest. A slot in the lid had allowed the generous to contribute as they desired, and, no doubt, a satisfying jingle rewarded the contributors. Once the fastener was removed, the lid could easily be lifted and completely removed to give easy access to the contents of the chest.

This ancient chest was just what was needed for collecting the money given by worshippers in the temple, so my father opened the chest and removed the lid. The chest was empty, except for a cloth lying at the bottom. For some reason, he ran his hand under the top board at the back of the chest, the board which normally held the lid in place, and felt something unexpected. It seemed to be a large piece of wood with a square cross-section

---

[2] 2 metres/6 feet

attached to the underside of the top board. Running his fingers from one end to the other, however, he found that there was a small gap between the square piece of wood and the side of the chest at one end. Not only that, but when he put his finger into the gap, he could feel a hole inside that square section – a hole to which he could feel no end.

His interest had been aroused, so he picked up one of the scattered items on the floor – it was a metal lamp-stand – and started to gently tap the puzzling piece of wood. Sure enough, it sounded slightly hollow. And sometimes when he tapped it, the fascinating lump of wood seemed almost to move a little.

By this time, the flicker of interest had become a fire of fascination for my father, and he had the chest carried outside so that he could examine it more carefully in the daylight.

Once outside, he continued his quest for understanding and found that if he grasped the hollow-seeming piece of wood and tried to wobble it, he could indeed move it very slightly, but none of his efforts seemed to achieve any greater freedom of movement. He tried tapping with the candlestick at the same time as trying to move the piece of wood backwards and forwards. Suddenly, there was a gentle thud as a small piece of wood dropped to the bottom of the chest, and the intriguing section of timber was able to move significantly. It still could not be removed, but it would move backwards and forwards, and even a little sideways at times.

It took my father a few minutes of methodical testing before suddenly the entire piece of wood came off in his hand and he felt its full weight, which was surprisingly heavy. Easing it out of the chest, he immediately looked at the open end and saw a cloth-wrapped object filling a circular hole in the wood. Tipping the object into his hand, he put down the heavy square section and began to unwrap the cloth. It was a linen cloth which seemed very old and a little stiff and dry, so my father unwrapped it very slowly and gently until the last layer came away, leaving a large scroll resting in his hand.

The skin of the scroll was darkened on the outside and had a look of great age, and the leather thong which held it closed also showed evidence of great age and frequent use at some time in the past. Clearly, however, it was many years since the thong had last been untied, and now it resisted any attempts to untie it. Finally, my father managed to loosen it enough to slide it gingerly off the end of the scroll, but these effects of age were a warning to be very careful with the scroll itself. Eagerly, but ever so gently, my father started to unroll the outer layers. By this time, there were a few Levites and priests watching, and the excitement was almost tangible as the treasure was uncovered. The first words were revealed, written in an old-fashioned script which my father read out, slowly and carefully to the listeners:

> "These are the words that Moses spoke to all Israel
> beyond the Jordan in the wilderness,
> in the Arabah opposite Suph,
> between Paran and Tophel, Laban,
> Hazeroth, and Dizahab.
> It is eleven days' journey from Horeb
> by the way of Mount Seir to Kadesh-barnea.
> In the fortieth year,
> on the first day of the eleventh month,
> Moses spoke to the people of Israel according to all
> that the Lord had given him
> in commandment to them."[3]

The words of Moses! Was this genuine? None of his audience had heard these words before, yet they were all

---

[3] Deuteronomy 1:1-3

thoroughly familiar with the words in the scrolls of scripture which were available to us. So what were these words? My father continued to read, despite the difficult script, going on with the story of Israel's departure from Sinai, the travel through the wilderness to the promised land and Israel's refusal to enter at the first opportunity. God's punishment and the people's response held my father's audience spellbound. This detail and the quick summary of the wilderness wanderings were all new to them. We now know of all these historical details from this record in the Book of the Law and some other discoveries made since, but only vague outlines had been known for many years before this wonderful discovery. Manasseh had torn the heart out of his nation's history. He had closed the eyes and ears of the people and then cut off the warning voice of God. What remained of the relationship? Only a distant memory of godliness that had lost its focus; a twisted presentation of God that lacked any edge. No wonder God was angry with us.

King Joash's wooden chest was taken out and placed at the entrance to the temple, and generous worshippers were encouraged to drop their donations into it. All of the earlier donations were in the possession of the gatekeepers of the temple, and Josiah sent some leading men to collect the money and count it with my father so that the refurbishment could begin straight away.

So it was that Shaphan and Maaseiah met with my father, the gatekeepers and other Levites to get the project going. Some of these men were organisers and administrators, while others were artisans who were eager to start work on the temple as soon as possible. The collected money was all counted, and experienced Levites were given the duty of estimating times and costs for the project. Overseers were appointed, and some of the artisans were given authority to begin work that very day – with money to buy urgently needed materials. Money was also given to the overseers who would find more craftsmen and others to fetch and carry. These men all had a mind to work and also felt the pressure of the king's expectations.

After the meeting, my father showed Shaphan the newly discovered scroll. Together they read it over, and to Shaphan's great credit, he was eager to take the scroll to King Josiah. What a change this was from the officious and over-cautious attitude that had led him, in the thirteenth year of King Josiah, to try to hide from King Josiah God's message through me – which had got him into trouble with his king[4].

Shaphan was a skilled scribe and adept at reading the old-fashioned script, so he took it to Josiah himself the next morning and read it to him, with some of his advisors listening also. This is easy to say, and you may not realise the magnitude of the job Shaphan had taken on or the commitment he expected from Josiah his king. Reading this book out loud takes about two and a half hours, once you are used to the different script and the various abbreviations that were used so long ago. If only I could have been there to hear it and to see Josiah's response! Not only did Josiah listen to the entire scroll, but his response showed a humility not seen in any of the previous kings of Judah or Israel. Despite being accustomed to kingship and to an almost fawning adoration from all around him throughout his life, Josiah's response to hearing God's law directly was one of guilty horror. As he heard God's words of blessings for obedience and curses for disobedience, he stood, tore his sumptuous robe and then sat down, not on his throne, but on the steps in front of Shaphan as he continued to read the words of Yahweh promising desolation for the nation.

---

[4] See Volume 1 – Early Days, Chapter 13

After listening through to the very end of the Book of the Law, Josiah rose.

"Can there be any doubt that this is the true word of Yahweh?" he asked Shaphan.

"I don't think so, my lord," replied Shaphan. "It sounds genuine, and it looks as if it had been hidden for many years. Hilkiah is also convinced that it is genuine."

Josiah sat down again on his throne, put his head in his hands and closed his eyes for a time. He was plainly deeply shaken by the words he had heard. There was a long silence in the throne room. Everyone there realised the importance of the message they had just heard. And everyone realised that Josiah must now provide leadership. He alone must lead his kingdom as a shepherd. But he was a shepherd for whom the rules had suddenly changed. He had just heard right and wrong defined in ways that he had never heard before, and very little of the right had been seen in the nation for almost a hundred years. Curses had been read in his ears which promised harsh punishments for the very behaviour he saw around him every day. What could he do? Where should he start? How would God want him to respond?

As a king, Josiah was humble, but decisive. He ordered that Hilkiah the High Priest be brought before him, along with all of his most trusted advisors, including Ahikam, Achbor and Asaiah. Once all were present and had heard a short explanation of the amazing discovery, he asked for parts of the scroll to be read again: details of God as the one and only God; special instructions for kings; Israel's annual feasts; and then particularly the short section of blessings for obedience, and the lengthier list of curses for disobedience.

"What do you think, Hilkiah?" Josiah asked, when these passages had been read again. "What should we do? What should I do as king?"

If only I could have been there for that monumental moment. It was vital for the kingdom and vital for my father as well. But I was in Rabbah of the Ammonites and all I could do was to read my father's letter and rejoice at the brief news it contained.

CR

God's work in Ammon had already kept me busy for two months, and I had previously expected to spend another month in the areas around Rabbah before heading south into Moab. Instead, just two days later, I was on my way home to Anathoth, eager to arrive as soon as possible. God had given me permission to return, and I would be able to spend some months there, during which time I might also have an opportunity to help with the newly accelerated reforms of Josiah.

Travelling west and a little south in the cool of early morning, I climbed to the top of the watershed before beginning the long descent toward the Jordan River. The hazy outlines of the mountains around Jerusalem stood tall above the deep rift of the Jordan valley. I had two days of stiff walking before me, but anticipation eased the strain and the road passed quickly under my feet.

In the afternoon of the following day I was walking up the road out of the Jordan valley from Jericho, climbing eagerly towards the hill country north of Jerusalem. As the steepness of the climb eased, I took the path to Anathoth while the heat of the afternoon cooled towards sunset. Thoughts of the newly-found Book of the Law had filled my head since crossing the Jordan River early that morning. What was this "Book of the Law" and where did it come from? If it was genuine, and everything I had heard from my father suggested that it was, what might now be achieved for reform in Judah?

Thoughts of my mother's food also claimed my attention. Despite my arrival being completely unexpected, I hoped that there would be enough of that special home-cooked food to fill a stomach used to, but not completely satisfied by, the varied food of other nations. My mother's cooking was still my favourite fare, and none of the special foreign dishes tasted half as good. My mouth was watering as I entered Anathoth and made my way along the familiar path to our home.

My welcome was all I could have hoped for. Recognising my call of "Shalom" as I approached the door, my mother hurried out and greeted me with a happy "Shalom," and a welcoming kiss.

My father followed more slowly, but also greeted me with a kiss. "The Lord be with you, Jeremiah," he said.

"The Lord bless you," I answered.

"Well, come in, my son," he responded, putting his arm around my shoulders. "We have much to talk about." His voice and his smile seemed more eager and purposeful than I remembered, and my heart leapt with hope. Reformation really was possible, and maybe the Book of the Law was the trigger God had provided.

We went inside together; the familiar smell of our house and the enticing aroma of the evening meal in the last stages of preparation filled my nostrils. It was good to be home.

Chapter 2

Home again

That night we sat and talked. Only my father and my mother were present, as the situation in our house had changed since I had left four and a half years before. Neither of my brothers lived at home any more. One year after I had left, my oldest brother Azariah had married and moved out. He now lived in a house of his own nearby in Anathoth with his wife Hephzibah and their two young sons Seraiah and Zadok. Another Zadok. Sometimes we Levites like to make things difficult for ourselves. Genealogies are so important to us, and yet we keep using the same names in many generations despite the confusion this causes. Zadok was the name of the priest who replaced Abiathar as High Priest in the times of King David and King Solomon when God fulfilled his promise to Eli that his family would not continue as priests before God[5]. Not

---

[5] 1 Samuel 2:30-36 and 1 Kings 2:27

only that, but my father's grandfather was also called Zadok. Funnily enough, Seraiah was the name of David's secretary when Zadok and Abiathar were priests in the time of King David[6]. We don't seem to want to learn from the difficulties the repeated use of names has already caused, and I'm sure it is going to cause great problems in our family tree sooner or later.

Unfortunately, I had not been able to attend Azariah's wedding. Far over to the east in Elam for a few months, I didn't even hear of the wedding until after it was all over. My brother never forgave me for that, although he was probably secretly glad that I wasn't there. No doubt his friends all expressed their sorrow that the future High Priest should be saddled with a crackpot prophet for a brother; and how could anyone celebrate properly with him around?

Gemariah had been married almost two years ago and I was away for his wedding too. That upset me. It was not until some time afterwards that I understood God's intentions in keeping me away from these celebrations, but more of that later. My mother reported that their firstborn, my young nephew Hasshub, was still recovering from a fever that had worried them all and suggested that I should go and visit them soon. Hasshub had been born two weeks before his cousin Zadok, but was a sickly child.

My first meal at home was delicious and my parents' company was a pleasure such as I had not enjoyed for a long time. Yet when I went to bed that night, tired with the days of walking, I felt that I had received both good and bad news.

---

[6] 2 Samuel 8:17

My father was very pleased to see me and very enthusiastic about his discovery in the temple. Josiah's plans for reform filled his conversation and he was excited to be involved. This was the good news.

The bad news was all in the little things. It was hard to put my finger on what was wrong, but I felt uneasy. The truth was that I no longer belonged. God had taken me out of my world and put me into another of his choosing.

Twenty-one years of age is too young to feel nostalgic, but so I felt that night. Oh, for the time when I was too young to be involved in the complexities of adult life; times when I had my place in the family, and fitted in happily.

The next morning came with a grey sky and the accustomed sounds of familiar birds as I went to my favourite hillside to pray and think. It was good to be back in my home environment, and I crept quietly out of the house and went to my rendezvous with God. Walking along the path, I wondered what would happen today. How would Jerusalem and her people have changed? I remembered their refusal to change in the thirteenth year of King Josiah and wondered whether they would be any different in this eighteenth year. Josiah was now twenty-five years old and all the reports I had heard of him were still overwhelmingly positive. His work of removing foreign idols had continued in Jerusalem as well as through parts of Judah and beyond, and he had finally started on the temple.

Why had Josiah taken so long to start working on the temple? I didn't know the answer myself, but I wondered whether it was because the temple had been more an empty shell, an appearance of worship, rather than a genuine centre for the living worship of Yahweh. Hezekiah had begun his reign by immediately starting work on purifying the temple[7]; Josiah had worked practically everywhere but the temple. In fact, the temple had been almost the last place Josiah had striven to purify. I pondered the question again, as I settled myself on a pile of stones in the early light of dawn: would his work elsewhere have been easier if he had attended to the temple first? The hillside on which I sat sloped down towards the east in front of me and the light from the east grew slowly stronger as I pondered this question.

Memories floated through my mind of the morning after my seventeenth birthday, more than four years before, when some unusual clouds had caught my attention and Yahweh had spoken to me. How much God had changed my life since that cold morning! But how much had Judah changed in that time? Would my nation have changed more if King Josiah had attended to the temple earlier? Day was coming, but there would be no glorious sunrise today, just a steady lightening under heavy grey clouds. Faint tinges of yellow coloured the horizon, but the sun was completely hidden from sight. As usual, I prayed for my family and my nation, praying that God's light would shine on their path in this time of reformation.

The Book of the Law – found at such a time of opportunity! Words from God to guide King Josiah. Surely it must be a sign that Josiah would succeed in turning Judah back to God? This was the thought that

---

[7] 2 Chronicles 29:3, 16-17

had recurred endlessly in my mind as I had walked towards Anathoth during the last two days. Yet the discussions of the previous night had undermined my confidence. What changes had I hoped to see in my father? He was clearly happy with the discovery of the Book of the Law: he had made arrangements for it to be widely copied, and already scribes were working away diligently, copying. It was frustrating that almost a week had been lost as various scribes squabbled over the plan for copying the precious scroll, but at least something was happening.

Maybe it was the lack of remorse that worried me, the absence of any feeling that the nation had sinned and ignored God's attempts to provide direction through the scripture or through prophets. The only remorse shown had been shown by Josiah – the one who probably had the least reason for it, based on his own behaviour. But I suspect it has always been that way.

I must read the Book of the Law. It could take some time before I would be able to, though, as there was only one copy available and the copying had only begun on the day I left Rabbah. Immer, my old teacher, had been placed in charge of the copying, and all of the available expert scribes would be working on the task. It was an important matter, a prestigious responsibility, given the urgent support of the king. This was what had slowed down the process. All of the senior scribes wanted the job, and the jockeying for position had wasted several days. Finally, Josiah himself had forced the issue by setting a deadline for the work to begin. He wanted the first copy for himself, but he had also commanded that it be part of a batch of 30 copies which he had ordered to be made at the same time. The number was fairly arbitrary, but Josiah did not want the Book of the Law to be lost again.

During the posturing and self-promotion of the scribes seeking these prominent positions, many scrolls had been displayed as examples of their work, and it had been noted that small parts of the text of the Book of the Law had actually been available already in other forms. This had triggered a deeper search which was still ongoing.

Again I wondered whether God's work for me might include such an undertaking: investigating the scriptures and other scrolls that were available and reviewing them. After all, we obviously needed to know which books could be relied on as words from God and which deserved no such respect. I had been hearing God's messages to various nations over a period of more than four years, and I had begun to feel that I was slowly learning to understand more of God's ways. I still often felt that God's thoughts were far beyond mine, but my understanding was growing. It was a feeling of reaching out towards God, stretching my mind up towards his and slowly, ever so slowly, climbing a ladder towards him. At times I felt as if I had slipped, and that there were more rungs above me than there had been before, while at other times I seemed to climb several rungs very quickly. But overall, it seemed that God was slowly and patiently teaching me. Maybe this knowledge would be useful in weeding out the worthless scrolls from the precious ones.

My thoughts and prayers continued as I tried to plan out the day before me. As a seventeen-year-old, prayer had been important to me, but prayer takes time to develop in life. We can never forget that God is perfectly pure, all-powerful and demanding. Yet he is also close to us if we reach out to him on his terms. For me, the last few years had made prayer become essential. Quite simply, I had to do God's work every day, and I could not know what that work was without prayer. Sometimes my prayers prompted direct responses from God, but even when they didn't, he would still work on my mind if I took the time to let him. If I didn't, because I was in too much of a hurry or too sure that I knew what was best, my days were still very busy, but they lost the guidance of God's hand. And I had found that life just did not work properly that way. Prayer took time, but it was a bit like getting some special equipment, putting on some armour, or getting a guide to walk beside me. I really couldn't do without it.

The light continued to strengthen as I prayed, and then it was time to return to the house. Morning had begun. My mind was filled with many possibilities, but there were some particular things I wanted to do more than others, and they would keep me busy enough for this day and probably for a few days to come.

A little misty rain was falling as I returned to the house, reminding me that we were at the end of the dry season. The harvest was over and during the next few months, the weather would become colder and rain more common. The greyness of the sky and the misty smear of rain spread a dullness over the scene which contrasted with the optimism that had filled Jerusalem and Anathoth and was spreading across the nation.

A little down the hill from our home I could see Azariah's house – another imposing stone building reflecting his position of importance in Judah. Our father was healthy and strong, but when he slept with his fathers, Azariah would be the next High Priest of Yahweh. I wondered how he felt about the newly discovered Book of the Law. I must visit today and see my two little nephews as well. So much had changed.

CR

Breakfast was a peaceful meal and my mother fussed around me as we shared our bread and enjoyed some dates and summer figs. Like a hen with only one chick, she pampered me and made me feel welcome. Since leaving to visit Israel four and a half years ago, my visits had been often unannounced and always fleeting, and my admission that I expected to stay for several months this time had filled her motherly heart with pleasure. For myself, I was looking forward to having more opportunities to discuss the events of the nation and the word of God with her. It would be like old times again.

My father obviously had plans for me, but it was clearly going to take some time before we got to speaking about them. He smiled as he reminisced about the time when I had told Immer my teacher about my new direction as a prophet of Yahweh, remembering some of the beautifully crafted put-downs I had reported.

"What were the words exactly, my son?" my father asked.

I had no difficulty remembering. "He said, 'A prophet, you say, young man? Ah, as a prophet you will have so much knowledge to dispense to the ignorant. How we will all benefit.'" Unconsciously, I imitated Immer's ponderous delivery and slightly nasal twang.

"That was the first one," I continued, "but the one that I have actually found very helpful was when he said, 'Prophets come to reform everyone else.' "

My father chuckled and I wondered if he agreed with Immer. He would never tell me so, but in his heart he probably did.

Immer's statements had hurt a lot at the time, but they had actually been quite helpful when I thought about them. His comments had helped me to probe my own attitudes and behaviour, and taught me to always try to apply God's words to myself first. I still have problems with pride, but Immer's pithy contempt has helped me more than he ever knew.

My father went on to tell me about how Immer had begun the work of copying the Book of the Law, and his explanation of the process showed me again how much I had to learn. One precious manuscript must be copied, quickly and accurately, to thirty new manuscripts as well as being updated to use modern characters, writing forms and abbreviations. The ancient scroll contained almost as many words as the scroll of Isaiah which I had carried around with me throughout my early work as a prophet. Such scrolls are made up of several pieces of animal skin, with the text written in beautifully neat columns. Using the standard size of writing, a scribe could fit about 1,500 words on such a piece of parchment, and that was the first step in the process that had been agreed.

The original scroll had been ever so carefully separated into sheets. The tiny stitches joining the individual pieces of parchment were cut and the threads unpicked until sixteen separate pieces of ancient parchment lay curled on the bench.

The plan was for sixteen of the best scribes to each copy the text from one sheet of the original scroll onto a new piece of parchment until they had finished. Each copy would be rigorously checked, first by the scribe who had copied it, then by Immer and ten other scribes, one after another. As far as possible, neither the original scroll nor the copy would be touched during the checking process so that no unnecessary wear would shorten the life of either scroll. Any errors that were found in the new copies would be assessed to decide whether they could be invisibly fixed or not. Since the very best scribes were being used for the work, very few errors were to be expected, but even experts make mistakes from time to time. In this batch of copies, it had been decided that if any sheet of parchment could not have all errors fixed invisibly using the best available methods, then the sheet would not be used in one of the final scrolls. If the errors could be easily fixed so that there would be no confusion for subsequent copiers, it could be used as an approved copy version – scribes could use it to copy from, but it would not be included in one of the finished scrolls ordered by King Josiah.

In this way, all sixteen sheets were being copied and updated at the same time without any loss of accuracy or reliability. But it would still take time. A careful scribe would take about two days to copy and check his sheet of parchment. A careful checker would take about another two or three hours to verify that the 1,500 words on the sheet matched in every character. Ten such checkers would consume three days of work – possibly four as the days grew shorter; good light is needed for good checking. The first copy made of each sheet would be more difficult to check because it must be checked against the original, while allowing for the updates being made to the characters and abbreviations. Once the validation of these was complete, the copy would be used as the basis for further copying.

According to my father, the copying and initial checking of the first sixteen sheets should have finished before sunset last night. Today, the detailed review by Immer and the other scribes would begin, and my father wanted to be there to witness the process and see the results. He also wanted me to come with him and I was eager to go – determined to find a way to read the text myself.

Throughout breakfast, my mother continued to make sure I was properly fed. She never believed that I was able to eat properly while I was away from home and was always deeply suspicious of foreign food. "They don't know how to prepare food properly," she fussed, "and you are always too easily distracted when other things are going on, so that you wouldn't even notice."

"Fruit doesn't require much preparation, mother," I replied mildly.

"Maybe not, but you can't eat fruit all day, let alone all year," she countered.

"…and they can't do much to make bread unclean," I continued.

"What if they mix in camel's milk? What if they let bugs grow in the flour and make the bread with them in it? That wouldn't be clean!"

"But nobody, not even foreigners, would want to eat bread cooked with bugs in it, mother," I said with a laugh.

"I'm not so sure," she muttered darkly, as she placed a loaf of her incomparable bread in my hands. "We all know that God gave us rules for a reason. After all, Gentiles are Gentiles."

I gave up the argument and enjoyed the food she plied me with. It tasted good, and my mother was right to some extent – it was good to be able to eat without needing to worry about whether or not the food was ritually clean.

But my mother wasn't interested only in food. She was clearly excited by the discovery of the Book of the Law and had obviously discussed with my father all that he could remember of its contents. He was one of the very few people who had had the opportunity to read all of the scroll, but his eyesight had been getting worse recently and he had found the reading hard work. The old-fashioned script hadn't helped either, and as a result, he didn't remember very much of the contents. He chiefly remembered the ten commandments, the blessings and curses, and a song of Moses from near the end.

One particular passage had stuck in his memory, and he had repeated it several times to my mother:

" 'You shall therefore lay up these words of mine
in your heart and in your soul,
and you shall bind them as a sign on your hand,
and they shall be as frontlets between your eyes.
You shall teach them to your children,
talking of them when you are sitting in your house,
and when you are walking by the way,
and when you lie down, and when you rise.
You shall write them on the doorposts of your house
and on your gates,
that your days and the days of your children

may be multiplied
in the land that the Lord swore
to your fathers to give them,
as long as the heavens are above the earth.'[8]"

"And that is just what we have done!" my father had exulted. "As a nation, we have laid up the words of Yahweh and taught them to our children. Even through the times of King Manasseh, we have still kept his Book of the Law. Oh, it is true that we lost access to it for a time, and King Josiah is right to be concerned about how exactly we have been applying God's law, but overall, as a nation, we have done rather well, I feel."

When my mother reported this to me as I ate my bread, I could hardly believe that anyone could be so breathtakingly smug and self-satisfied. Still, I had been away for a long time. Maybe the nation had genuinely turned back to God and would truly follow these instructions from now on. But there was no question in my mind that we hadn't been doing so previously, and it seemed as if Josiah agreed with me, for had he not responded with shock and horror when he heard of God's requirements – and his judgements?

Nevertheless, I managed to hide my incredulity, and even to reserve judgement to some extent. I would wait until I saw the mood of the nation now. I was also desperately eager to find out what it was in the Book of the Law of Yahweh that had upset Josiah so much.

---

[8] Deuteronomy 11:18-21

Chapter 3

Return to Jerusalem

The brief shower of early morning had passed, and the sun had driven away the grey clouds. Shortly after breakfast, my father and I took the road to Jerusalem. My father was still well able to walk the path, but he had aged noticeably while I was away. His steps were a little slower, and each was more cautious. He used his staff more carefully and seemed to rely on its support at times. His voice was still full-bodied and smooth, caressing the ear with its deep richness, but I noticed that its delivery was a little slower.

At first, we walked in silence down the familiar path, past the flat rock on which, in the depths of a cold spring night during the thirteenth year of King Josiah, some of my questions about God's expectations had been untangled. It had been such a struggle to understand why God's message to a good king had been so uncompromisingly critical of the kingdom of Judah. My conclusion, that Josiah had received such a message because he would listen and try to do something, had guided my understanding of God from then on. God expects everything that we can possibly give him, but not more. Simple warnings and words of condemnation had been sent to Manasseh by God through prophets, but much more detailed messages had been sent to Hezekiah through several prophets, and now Josiah could also benefit from such detailed messages.

These thoughts were running through my mind only: my father wanted to speak about the future of the family.

"My son," he ventured, "your brothers are both busy with the work God gave us as descendants of Aaron. Azariah was ordained two years ago and will take over from me as High Priest when I die. Gemariah is doing his work as a Levite and preparing for the time when he can be ordained also. They are both married and have both been blessed with sons."

I thought that I could see where this discussion was leading and I wasn't completely averse to it, as long as my father wasn't going to force one of his favoured girls on me. Into my mind's eye flashed a sudden picture of long flowing hair framing a quietly smiling face, while my ears relived the delight of a beautiful lilting voice singing the wonderful words of David amidst the bustle and hurry of that surprising inn in Bethel. The slim owner of that beautiful voice had often been in my thoughts during my travels.

"But what about you, my son?" my father continued. "You cannot keep wandering around visiting exotic capitals forever, you know." My father never did understand that it was not the travel or the exotic destinations that led me to visit other countries. In fact, I often longed for the quiet life of home and family, of worship and study. But these were not part of the script God had written for me, and surely my maker would know what was best for me?

"What do you mean, father?" Delaying tactics might extract more information before I had to commit myself to anything.

"You are almost 22 years old now, and I would feel happier if all my sons were taken care of, each provided with a good wife to fill his years with happiness. I know that both Azariah and Gemariah were a few years older than you are when they married, but this is a time of peace and security and one can never tell when that might end. It is better to have a wife than to want one. I was your age when I was betrothed, and it was a time of great uncertainty for us all, with King Manasseh reigning. Your mother's family moved away from Jerusalem to Anathoth shortly after Manasseh became king and they were not popular with the king or his men. That was a long time before your mother was born – or I, myself, for that matter. Marrying her was probably the bravest thing I ever did," he mused, and a smile played around the corners of his mouth. "She was only seventeen when we were betrothed and eighteen when we married, but she has always been a woman of faith, your mother. My own father was a little edgy about me marrying her. A dangerous family to associate with, he said: her father was a little too outspoken, you know. Shortly after our marriage, they moved as far south from Jerusalem as they could go, and the family still lives there. Oh, life can be difficult. Maybe if I had been braver, we could have...."

He looked a little wistful as his voice trailed off and I was reminded again that people are not always simple to understand. My father liked the idea of an unbending faith – at least in theory. But religion had always been a job for him, and when conflicts arose, he would take the path of least resistance to the most visible opposition. The idea of holding a path of faith and certainty against all opposition was a bit of a dream to him; an unattainable dream. He liked the idea to some extent, but comfort and riches had an immediate attraction which obscured the long-term happiness of trust in God.

Again we walked for some minutes in silence, and I thought, with surprise, that my father was indulging in the nostalgia that comes with advancing age. This, along with my observations about his care in walking, made me pause and think. How old was he? He couldn't be that old: he had been 22 when he was married, and Azariah had been born one year later and was now 31 years old. So my father must be 54 years old. Not young, but certainly not old. In the past, the descendants of Levi had often been very long-lived, living to more than twice my father's current age, but recent generations hadn't lasted so long.

As we walked around the flank of a hill, we approached a small grove of trees, one of the last sections of the path still visible from Anathoth. The path passed for a short distance through the lower parts of this grove as it spread untidily down the hillside. This grove was a place of pleasant memories for me. A place in which I had played with friends, happily climbing trees together in that carefree period of life before responsibility lays its heavy hand upon you. I was thinking of my friends – particularly Adaiah, Chelub and Benaiah – as we passed the first tree, and then I saw it. There, sitting underneath the tree, its short round body looking more like an oversized egg than an irresistible symbol of supernatural power, was an idol. Nestled against the hillside, its short stubby arms protruded impotently from its side and its painted face leered at us.

"When did this come here?" I demanded, and I could not keep the harsh disgust from my voice.

"It was put here about a year ago, just after your last visit," my father replied. "Josiah has been clearing Jerusalem of idols, and so people have been moving them to places like this to keep them out of his sight." I took a step towards the idol and my father said hurriedly, "Of course, they don't want to upset the king, so it is better this way."

I ignored the attempted justification and strode the few furious strides needed to bring the abominable image within reach. The arms I used, first as handles to lift it from its pathetic resting place, and then to provide extra leverage as I hurled it towards the unforgiving ground. The hideous plaster figurine struck the path, bounced, and rolled, both arms shearing off, the straw with which it was stuffed protruding through the shattered surface.

It came to rest against a tree and I immediately picked up a branch that was lying nearby and used it to beat the damaged deity into ever smaller pieces.

"How has this been allowed to stay here?" I asked once I had finished, breathing a little heavily.

"I believe that some of the men of Anathoth look after it and even provide the offerings," he waved his hand to a bowl lying near the original resting place of the egg-shaped image. "They won't be pleased," he warned. He didn't look pleased himself.

"What else could I have done, father?" I enquired.

"You could have just left it alone!" he answered, sounding a little concerned and upset. "It wasn't hurting you, and it wasn't yours to destroy." He looked around as if to check that no-one had seen my action. "You've gone too far this time, Jeremiah," he finished.

"This land is Yahweh's land," I argued. "Idols make the land unclean. They hurt the land, they hurt you and they hurt me. This is exactly why God plans to destroy the land. Our only hope of avoiding that destruction is to eradicate these cursed idols." The stick was still in my hand and I swung it again at the jumble of plaster and straw that lay beside the dusty path. "Yahweh is a jealous

God," I continued. "Didn't the Book of the Law tell you that?"

"I suppose it did," he muttered, "but surely it just means that he doesn't want us to reject him as our God. We have not gone after the Baals, but as a nation, we have always been tolerant and patient with foreigners, including their gods."

"Too patient," I observed, "and too willing to learn to worship the same gods."

"Well, Jeremiah," my father was recovering his poise after the unexpected destruction of an idol he had been accustomed to tolerating, "what you've done here isn't going to make people happy."

I didn't answer, reflecting that he was probably right.

Cresting the saddle between Har Hatsophim and the Mount of Olives, we looked down on Jerusalem. My eyes were immediately drawn to the temple, and the changes amazed me. The two bronze pillars at the entrance to the temple had been cleaned! Decades of bird droppings had been removed and the burnished bronze of the pillars gleamed in the sun. I had known that work was to be done on God's temple, but it surprised me how much I reacted to the change. I felt a surge of joy and hopefulness. Maybe, just maybe, the nation could find true repentance and focus their minds on God.

A more careful look at the temple, even from that distance, showed that there was still much to be done to make the appearance of the temple compare with the splendour of the king's palace, but it also showed that the temple was swarming with workers. Scaffolding clung precariously to various parts of the building and it was clear that the cleaning of the stonework was well underway. I was no stonemason and had no idea how they would manage it, but it looked as if some of the stones were being replaced in various places.

My father watched my reactions and smiled broadly at me. "The work is going on well, isn't it? Look what we are doing with the temple, my son. Surely God will be pleased with this?"

℘

Walking down into the valley of the Kidron, I felt much happier – probably happier than I had felt since my seventeenth birthday. My mind was buzzing with the hope of complete reform in my nation. King Josiah was leading his sheep to God, and everything would be alright. This must be the reason why God had not given me that depressing message he had given to Isaiah, spelling out how long his job would continue: "Until the cities lie desolate and without inhabitant."[9] Obviously, my job was to be successful, and Judah would repent, turning to God with complete honesty.

It is amazing how quickly one can forget things – my horror at finding an idol in one of the preferred haunts of my childhood had been forgotten in this euphoria of hope and optimism. I suppose hope and optimism make for a happier life.

Not much had changed about the approaches to the city from the first day of my work as a prophet. Market stalls still lined the road to the walls and sheep and goats still bleated from their pens, competing with the shouts encouraging us to buy. Yet it seemed to me that there was a difference too. There seemed to be a feeling of suppressed excitement, a sense that something important was happening. Some of the shouted messages were quite

---

9 Isaiah 6:11

different. There was much more encouragement for us to buy "lambs without blemish" as offerings to Yahweh. The name of God was to be heard much more, often being used to back up a trader's claim of quality. I wasn't sure that this was what God had intended when he told us to take our oaths in his name, and I found myself rather uncomfortable with this free use of his name in trade.

However, it was certainly good that the names of Baal, Asherah, Milcom and all the other gods were heard less frequently than had been the case in that spring of the thirteenth year of Josiah when I had begun my work as a prophet. At the same time, there were still many references to these gods mixed in with the blithe use of Yahweh's name.

Of course, my father was not wearing his special High Priest's clothes, but many people still recognised him and he was treated with great respect. "Shalom," many said, while others said, "The Lord bless you," or "The Lord be with you." But there were also others who greeted him with "Baal's blessings," or "Molech mark you," and my father responded in kind.

I don't know of any way to express my utter disbelief when I heard this. The first time, I was certain I must have misheard, but repetition removed that possibility. And then I simply could not believe what I was hearing. This man, my father, was High Priest to Yahweh, the only living God – yet here he was, exchanging greetings which invoked the names of dead idols!

Where can I start in expressing the horror and outrage I felt? From a purely legal point of view, these gods were all but illegal. Josiah had outlawed the maintenance of priests and altars for the worship of Baal, Asherah and the rest, though I grudgingly admitted to myself that he had not explicitly forbidden the use of their names in casual conversation.

As these thoughts raced furiously through my mind, I stopped. I had been angry when we came across the idol on the road, but that was nothing compared with the burning anger I felt now. And then came the familiar fire of the word of the Lord within me. Words he had planted in my mind some four and a half years before boiled up and then burst from me as my father stopped, turned around, and looked at me enquiringly:

> " 'How can you say, "I am not unclean,
> I have not gone after the Baals"?
> Look at your way in the valley;
> know what you have done —
> a restless young camel running here and there,
> a wild donkey used to the wilderness,
> in her heat sniffing the wind!
> Who can restrain her lust?
> None who seek her need weary themselves;
> in her month they will find her.
> Keep your feet from going unshod
> and your throat from thirst.
> But you said, "It is hopeless, for I have loved foreigners,
> and after them I will go." ' "

My father was looking bewildered, but God's words continued tumbling out of me:

> " 'As a thief is shamed when caught,
> so the house of Israel shall be shamed:
> they, their kings, their officials,
> their priests, and their prophets,
> who say to a tree, "You are my father,"
> and to a stone, "You gave me birth."
> For they have turned their back to me,
> and not their face.'[10]"

---

[10] Jeremiah 2:23-27

The irresistible hand that kept me speaking softened its grip a little and I stopped. Short of breath and flustered, I thought of the only other time God had forced me to speak. It too had been to my father, on the night when I had first read the smelly scroll of Isaiah. That occasion had been a shock to me – and an even greater shock to my father. As on that occasion, the fire of God stayed burning brightly afterwards, igniting a desire to do something, but no longer actually compelling me to speak. The words glowed, flickered, flamed in my mind's eye, commanding my attention and threatening to break out again. I was no longer angry. Instead I was overcome; speechless. What had I done? Of course, reasoned thought would have told me that it was not I who had done it, but emotional reactions do not pause for thought, or even welcome thought when it comes. Rational thought later told me that these two occasions had clearly answered one of my long-standing questions about my work for God: Was it right to go against the wishes of my father? Shouldn't I show respect for my father? The work of Yahweh had answered the question by forcing me to speak, speaking words which did not show the respect a son was expected to show his father. Later I would be able take some comfort from this, but at the time all I could do was stare at my father. I suspect that my mouth was also hanging open a little.

There was no way that this outburst could be smoothed over. The people who had greeted my father with a reference to Baal were still within earshot and had stopped when they heard my words. My voice has a tendency to carry and many people seemed to have heard what I said. Twenty or thirty people had stopped and were watching curiously, eager to see what would happen. One or two did not want to wait; they wanted to make something happen.

"Is that how you speak to God's High Priest, young man?" said one, looking at me threateningly.

His friend whispered something in his ear, and the man looked outraged. I guessed that his friend had recognised me as my father's son and apprised him of the fact.

"Are you really the son of Hilkiah, our High Priest?" he asked.

"Yes," I answered. I couldn't think of anything else to say.

"Haven't you ever learned respect? Respect for your father, respect for God's High Priest?" he continued.

What should I say? God had inspired this attack on his High Priest, this lack of respect in a son, so I must not water it down; but where would all of this lead? "Respect for Yahweh our God must come first," I stated. "We are God's chosen people. He chose us and gave us a land flowing with milk and honey, yet we have rejected him by allowing Baal and Asherah to stay in the land. This is what Yahweh our God says:

> " 'If you return, O Israel, declares the Lord,
> to me you should return.
> If you remove your detestable things from my presence,
> and do not waver,
> and if you swear, "As the Lord lives,"
> in truth, in justice, and in righteousness,
> then nations shall bless themselves in him,
> and in him shall they glory.'[11] "

"But how can we return to God?" the man demanded. "We have not left him! We have the temple of the Lord, we have his High Priest; what more could you ask for?"

---

[11] Jeremiah 4:1-2

"Yahweh, our God, asks for faithfulness," I responded, "yet the names of other gods pour out of our mouths. Return to God and do not waver between him and these dead idols. When we follow worthless things, we become worthless."

More than four years of speaking God's words had taught me to answer the questions of listeners by using as many of Yahweh's words as possible, while still answering the question directly. God had given me many words to work with and continued to guide me in choosing which ones to use. Nevertheless, the answer I gave did not satisfy this particular questioner.

"Are you saying that God's High Priest has become worthless? And you say this of your own father?" He spat out the words angrily and both he and his friend took a hostile step or two towards me.

It was clear that I was back in Judah! Four years of travelling around in different pagan, idolatrous nations had never felt so dangerous as being back in Jerusalem did. Other nations would listen to the message of Yahweh, but my nation wouldn't.

Meanwhile, my father remained standing where he was, a short distance away from me. He offered no protection; he made no attempt to calm the situation or to support me in any way. I was on my own. The only one with me was God, who had assured me that he would be with me as long as I did not cower before my opponents, and this I had learned, although it had not been easy.

"These are not my words, but Yahweh's," I repeated, standing firm in the face of the glowering, belligerent crowd. "When Yahweh speaks, we should listen. Weigh his words and ponder them – for in them you will find truth. If God says we have become worthless in his eyes, then follow the lead of King Josiah by trying to find out what we can do to become valuable to him again." The two leaders in aggression had simmered down a little and I turned away from them somewhat to speak to a larger audience. I spoke louder, "The Book of the Law of Yahweh has been found. I'm sure King Josiah will make sure it is read to all the people. Listen to God's law as your king has."

"But when can we hear the law?" a man asked.

"Ask your king and your priests," I responded, and waved towards my father. "Priests are to teach God's law. Ask them to do so!"

The look my father gave me was not the look of one eager to take an opportunity that suddenly opens in front of him. It was a look of irritation mixed with uncertainty. I suddenly remembered some of the early words God had spoken to me: "Those who handle the law did not know me."[12] It was true. My father, the High Priest, did not know Yahweh, or his law.

King Manasseh had achieved his goal.

---

[12] Jeremiah 2:8

Chapter 4

The Book of the Law

Within the temple area, a large room had been reserved for copying the Book of the Law. My father led me in without a word, preserving the frosty silence that had existed between us since the confrontation near the city gate. Large window areas allowed daylight to fall on the long tables at which several scribes sat busily working. The initial impression was one of complete concentration and utter silence, but after standing for some minutes watching, one could hear the scratching of pen nibs as the ink was swiftly and skilfully applied to the large sheet of parchment lying in front of each scribe. In one corner of the room, other scribes worked with sharpened knives, preparing pens for use. Others were mixing ink ready for use, a process I knew well, as all Levites were taught that necessary skill. Various different types of ink were used, depending on the writing surface being used. Using the wrong type of ink was an easy mistake to make, but one that would reduce the life of the work. As this was an important project, the people chosen for the work were the best available – not the sort of people who would make such a fundamental error as using the wrong ink.

In the opinion of Josiah our king, this was the most important project in the kingdom at present. King Josiah wanted those copies of the Book of the Law, and he wanted them quickly. His copy was to be the first one finished, and apparently he came every afternoon to check on progress, reading some of the work that had been completed since his last visit. There could have been no better way of making sure that the work progressed as quickly as possible. And knowing that the king might read their work inspired great care.

Beside one wall, a table was elevated above the others on a small platform, so that the man seated at the table commanded a view of the other tables and could observe the work being done. As we entered the room, this man was busily poring over a sheet of parchment, and it took some time before he looked up and noticed us. It was Immer, my former teacher, now appointed leader of this prestigious enterprise. He greeted my father warmly before turning to me and saying, "Ah, Jeremiah, you have returned to grace us with your presence once more. Have all the nations repented, so that now you return to straighten us out too?"

"I have returned because of the joyful news of the discovery of the Book of the Law," I replied, ignoring the snide remarks. "You have a wonderful work to do for the nation."

"Yes," he replied, "the king wants his book and the king shall have his book. As we speak, the Validators are checking." He waved his arm towards several tables at one end of the room, where many scribes were sitting in pairs, each with two sheets of parchment in front of them, obviously comparing the darker sheet of the original scroll with the new, lighter coloured sheet that had been copied over the last few days. "Already," he continued, "we have found some errors, and one particular sheet has been reassigned with determined misreads."

What his "scribe-speak" meant was that one sheet had errors that could not be corrected invisibly, so it had been marked as an invalid copy. Corrections would still be made to the sheet, but it would never be included in a final scroll. Instead, it would be kept for copying or teaching purposes. The scribe who had produced this failed copy was never named, of course, but I noticed Immer's eyes straying to the far corner of the room as he spoke of the condemned sheet, and the scribe hunched in that corner seemed to squirm a little under his gaze. Another such failure and the scribe would probably be reassigned himself. For the moment, however, he had been banished to a corner, and some swift and exquisite scribe-work would be required to worm his way back into Immer's favour. I was glad it was not me, for my writing had never really been up to scratch for an expert scribe.

"Listen to this, young Jeremiah," Immer said as he looked down at the sheet of parchment he had been checking:

> " 'I will raise up for them a prophet like you
> from among their brothers.
> And I will put my words in his mouth,
> and he shall speak to them all that I command him.' [13]

"Is that you, Jeremiah? Are you this prophet like Moses? Should we be honouring you like Moses? The new Moses, come down from Mount Sinai with words from Yahweh!"

Immer was speaking with cold sarcasm, but his words brought me up short because they fitted exactly with what God had said to me: "I have put my words in your

---

[13] Deuteronomy 18:18

mouth"[14] and "whatever I command you, you shall speak"[15]. Here was yet another reason why I must read this Book of the Law. I couldn't really believe that God would have given a prophecy about me, but then again, he had also said:

> "Before I formed you in the womb I knew you,
>   and before you were born I consecrated you;
>   I appointed you a prophet to the nations."[16]

Could I be this prophet? At the time, the whole idea seemed incredible, even the concept an impossible burden. This burden was to weigh me down for some time.

As Immer appeared ready to continue with his sneering contempt, my father interrupted and asked how the copying work was progressing.

Immer gave us a quick summary, reporting that all sixteen sheets had been copied once. The sixteen select scribes had each checked their own work, then Immer had briefly scanned each copy before passing it on to a pool of Validators – scribes especially skilled in the task of verifying the copying work of other scribes. All of the copied sheets were now being checked against the originals by the Validators – except for the condemned sheet which was now being recopied by the erring scribe. Once again, Immer's eyes strayed to the corner and the scribe squirmed anew.

The senior priests and scribes had taken the decision to update the scroll so that the new copies would use modern characters and abbreviations rather than the ancient style used in the scroll found in the temple. As a result, the copying and checking jobs were much more

---

[14] Jeremiah 1:9
[15] Jeremiah 1:7
[16] Jeremiah 1:5

difficult for this very first copy of each sheet. To make the job easier for the Validators, the scribes who had copied the sheets would help with the validation of the first copy. Any disagreements which could not be sorted out between the individual scribes and Validators would be reviewed by a committee of priests and scribes.

My father and Immer continued with a lengthy discussion of the complex scheduling required for the project, the current availability and quality of parchment, the quantities of ink that were needed, and many other practical details. I listened politely, but it was not what I was interested in at all. What about the *message* of the Book of the Law? My father had reported that Josiah had torn his clothes and wept, but he could not really explain to me why.

After these discussions had continued for what seemed like an interminable time, I gave up and turned to leave. It was clear that I was not going to get any opportunity to read the Book of the Law then. Immer and my father were so engrossed in their planning that they didn't even notice my departure. As I left, I saw that the disgraced scribe in the corner was busy with his scraping knife and hoped that he had not made another slip up. This one could easily be unforgivable.

❧

Outside in the precincts of the temple, I looked around for someone to ask where I could find Shallum, the son of Tikvah. He was keeper of the king's wardrobe, a part of the palace which was right next to the temple. He was also the husband of Huldah, the prophetess whom I had found so helpful when starting my work for Yahweh. I wanted to speak to him about what had happened when King Josiah's men had visited her, and to arrange a visit of my own if possible.

I was not very familiar with the temple area, having first been too young to be involved in any of the work of the temple and then too busy with other work which took me away from Jerusalem. Walking towards the gate, I had to pass a building, the door of which was slightly ajar. This door caught my attention, and I hesitated, hearing the sound of women's voices coming from within. This seemed a little strange to me, since most of the work in the temple was to be done by men. Nevertheless, I figured that these women should be able to tell me about Shallum the son of Tikvah, so I tapped on the door and pushed it open a little, looking around the door into the room. Spread around the room were looms on which brightly coloured material was being woven into hangings. Other colourful material was being embroidered with designs which I recognised, despite them being incomplete. The women turned and looked at me as the door opened, and the voices fell silent. Several drew in their breath quickly and one even said, "You!" as I opened the door a little further.

"Does anyone know where I can find Shallum the son of Tikvah, the son of Harhas?" I asked.

One of the women near me was hastily folding up her work, but it was too late. I had already seen the design she was working on. One or two others had turned their work upside down, but again, it was too late. The pictures of brazen nudity and sexual perversion had already caught my attention, and similar ones were also hung on the wall anyway, depicting all sorts of vile behaviour.

Another woman near the back of the room stood up and walked towards me. She did not look shy or diffident in any way. Her movements were more akin to the gliding steps of a predatory animal stalking its prey. Never taking her eyes off me, she moved seductively past the looms and piles of material as she said alluringly, "Come to see what really happens in the temple of Yahweh, have you? Young men like you are always welcome here."

The other women were exchanging looks and relaxing a little; they had obviously seen her in action before. Walking past the last stack of material, she… but I won't go into any more detail: suffice it to say that she was the sort of woman who revelled in leading innocents into the ways of death. I quickly turned and fled from the doorway, pulling the door closed behind me.

Running away from a woman is not something that any young man finds it easy to do, for more than one reason. All young men who have lived since the time of Joseph the son of Jacob are blessed beyond words by his example if they have heard of his escape from Potiphar's wife. Joseph ran away, and I have found his example to be my own salvation on more than one occasion. Some women are deadly dangerous, and running away is better than staying, trying to use logic, and ending up losing the fight with yourself.

I hurried, shaking, along a walkway into another building which lay between me and the gate of the temple area. Inside, I walked more slowly along the corridor, passing several doorways, but no longer having the courage to enquire of anyone who might be inside. Instead, I would leave God's temple and find somewhere safer to seek information. Through the doorway in front of me, I could see the temple gates leading down towards the palace and I began to feel a little more secure; that is, until I heard some soft but hurried footsteps behind me. Suddenly a woman's hand grabbed my arm and a sultry voice spoke in my ear. Instantly I pulled my arm free and ran. Down the corridor, through the doorway, across the courtyard and out through the gates of the temple.

I had escaped. Escaped from Yahweh's temple.

What a topsy-turvy morning it had been! From the pleasure of early morning meditation to overwhelming anger at idolatry; from embarrassment at Immer's sarcasm to irritation at his misdirected priorities; and now I was running from God's house to escape a rapacious woman.

Why was she there? What did she do in the temple? Having seen some of her behaviour, it didn't take much thought to be able to guess what she did. But in Yahweh's temple? The temple where my father was the High Priest?

What should I do? What could I do? Clearly I must speak to my father, but surely he must be unaware of it? And really, what was it all about anyway? The women, all of them – why were they there? They had been making wall hangings for idols in the temple of Yahweh; embroidering pictures of Asherah and the symbols of Baal on them; weaving mats with depictions of the depraved worship common to these disgusting idols. These actions would be horrible enough anywhere in Jerusalem, but in God's temple? In my excessive self-confidence and naiveté, I had thought that I understood how bad things were in Judah, but this morning had opened my eyes a little more to the true situation. It made me feel like a foreigner in my own country, one who does not understand the most basic mores of society.

When God had first called me in the thirteenth year of Josiah, I had known that the temple was used for more than just the worship of Yahweh. I had known of there being idols in the temple, but there were so many idols around in Judah that one became completely matter-of-fact about seeing them. We didn't even notice them, so used were we to ignoring them. To some extent, my shock now was just the difference between knowing something in theory and actually seeing it. I had heard of terrible things being done in the temple, too, but that was several years ago. I had been busy since then, and knew that King Josiah had also been busy removing idols and their worship from the land. The terrible stories had more or less slipped my mind over the intervening time, since I had never seen any of it for myself, but this morning's experience had brought it all back and made it horribly real.

I was shocked and felt completely lost. Had I been living in a fairyland, completely fooling myself? Did anyone in the temple worship God? Did anyone in Jerusalem even know God at all? Or were they all right, and I was wrong?

When you are shaken up enough, you start to question everything for a while. The feeling has come to me a few times, each of them a horrendous occasion in which my eyes have been opened a little further to see just how debased we humans really are – and how impervious human nature is to positive change. Fortunately, that sort of complete confusion doesn't last long – at least it never has for me.

It was about half an hour later that I started to come out of my state of utter shock and complete disillusionment. Seated on a low wall outside the temple of Yahweh, I started to go back to basics to unravel the confused tangle into which life seemed to have wound itself. God was real. I was sure of that. He had spoken within me; shown me signs; even taken me over at times. In him, I had an immovable foundation.

What next? My family? They were close to me, and I knew them all well, but where did they fit in with Yahweh, the God who was a real, living God? Did my father know about those women, weaving in the temple of Yahweh? I hoped that he didn't, that someone else had let them in for some activity or event that morning. But they had looked much too much at home, and the hangings on the walls had matched the hangings they were making. That woman, in particular, had not behaved like an unfamiliar visitor to the temple. No, she had looked comfortable, confident, completely at home, a skilled worker – and used to certain types of visitors. She had easily followed me through the corridors of the temple. I thought of the many times when I had prayed to God, arguing that my nation was not really bad enough to warrant his complete and categoric, not to mention irreversible, condemnation. But now? How could I pray for my nation now?

My own father had censured me for the criticism of my family when he heard God's words against the priests. Yet all the time, he had known this…. No, wait; I must not jump to conclusions. It was still faintly possible that he did not know about these women or their work. Yet they had not been concerned about being discovered; the door had been left ajar and their voices were not quiet….

I stood and walked towards the guards at the gate of the palace. Yes, Shallum the son of Tikvah was known by the guards and he was certainly in the palace, supervising some minor building works in the area called the king's wardrobe. One of them went to find him for me. My mind was still in turmoil and I felt that it would take some time to decide what to do next.

Gathering my thoughts and trying to gain some perspective on the day's events, it struck me that it was still morning. The sun's shadows still grew from the eastern walls of the king's courtyard and the temperature was still climbing as the autumn sun rose towards its zenith. Much had already happened, but there were still many hours left in the day, and in those hours I must see what could be done about the knowledge I now possessed.

The guardhouse near which I stood still offered a little shade, so I walked over and leaned against the wall. Taking a deep breath, I tried to stop, or at least slow, the turbulent jumble of my thoughts.

What had I actually learned this morning? While waiting for the guard to return, I took the opportunity to reconsider the words of God. Every word he had ever spoken to me still stood out clearly, from the very first words of his call to his most recent words to me about Ammon. It's not easy to describe how these words were available in my mind. The closest description is still to say that they are like writing on a wall, glowing writing that can flare up or glow more gently, depending on events. Words that are more relevant glow more brightly, but normally I will only see them if I choose to. Most of the time, I can ignore them all if I choose, and when I am agitated, they are sometimes obscured until I slow down. Try to imagine a scroll just off to one side of your sight, not intruding on your vision, not demanding your attention, but available whenever you want it. This is the best description I can give of the way the words of God are written in my mind.

So I scanned God's words in my mind. Words against many nations glowed back at me: some messages of final condemnation, other messages of temporary punishment, but very few words of hope. Scanning took longer now, and if I did not concentrate, the brighter glow of the words that were most relevant to the current situation would be lost. Not one of the words themselves was ever lost, either then or later, but it seemed to me that God was gradually asking more of me, more concentration, more meditation on his words. I had found it to be quite a simple rule: think more about God's words and they become easier to individually distinguish and understand – the immediate glow of "relevance" becomes much easier to see.

Many of the early words of God were glowing, with the brightest being the very ones I had spoken to my father earlier in the day, and it wasn't hard to see why. Judah believed itself to be God's people, clean in his sight, yet God's view was very different. In Yahweh's view, we had turned our back to him and not our face; we had done all the evil that we could find to do, and been very inventive about it, too. As I pondered these words and all the others that glowed particularly brightly, it became very clear that God knew exactly what was happening in his temple. "Well, of course!" you might say, and you would be right, but it took me a while to make that obvious link.

The temple of God, home to the worship of idols – what a horrible thing! But what could I do? What would God expect me to do?

Chapter 5

Shallum and Huldah

What makes someone take the path of a prophet or prophetess of Yahweh? For a genuine prophet, it is no glamorous job. The messages are almost always unwanted by the hearers, and so they often lead to the prophet being completely rejected by the audience. At least a prophet who is not genuine can choose his own message! Such "prophets" are often quite popular – but they know from the start that they are frauds, and who would want to get popularity by fraud? I would never have dared to falsely claim to be presenting God's words when I knew I was lying!

At that time, I knew in a general way that there were many people in Judah who claimed to be prophets of Yahweh, but I had not met any except Huldah, and she was undoubtedly genuine. However, God's words to me had made it clear that there had been, and still were, many false prophets.[17] These apparently set themselves up as

---

[17] Jeremiah 2:8, 26

messengers of many gods, prophesying by Baal or Asherah or Yahweh as the fancy took them. King Josiah would, no doubt, have known of such "prophets", but he had chosen to send to Huldah instead. I was glad, because I knew that Huldah was a genuine prophetess of Yahweh. But I also wanted to hear from her what had happened.

Back in the thirteenth year of Josiah, I had found her so encouraging when everyone else had seemed to want to take me away from God's work. At that time, my father had indicated that Huldah was not in favour in the palace, yet now King Josiah had sent to her to seek God's judgement. Obviously, King Josiah must now consider her more reliable than any of the other prophets he could have asked.

After a while, the guard returned and told me that Shallum was busy, but would come as soon as he could.

I continued to wait for quite a long time, wondering what I should do with my new knowledge about the temple. King Josiah needed to hear about it, but first I must speak to my father. I wanted to give him the opportunity to explain the situation first, or even to tell me that he was ignorant of it – although this seemed unlikely. As I waited, the shadow of the guardhouse gradually shrank as the sun climbed in the sky. By the time Shallum came out of one of the side entrances of the palace, there was no shade left and the sun was hot. He greeted me with an easy, "Shalom, Jeremiah. It has been a long time since we met. Can you come with me to my home?" He gestured with his hand towards the street outside the courtyard. I greeted him and nodded assent, and we walked past the guards and along the street towards the second quarter of Jerusalem.

As we walked, Shallum and I discussed the recent events in Jerusalem. He was pleased that his wife was finally receiving the respect she deserved from the palace.

In his mind, it was Josiah who was responsible for this change, not the nobles. Although they had known Huldah and her calling as a prophetess of Yahweh, they had never suggested to the king that he could find answers from God through her. In fact, Shallum was convinced that it was his own words to King Josiah that had brought about the change. A year or two before, King Josiah had been examining his wardrobe to see whether anything could be done to reduce its contents, as they simply took up too much space. Something had to change, and so Josiah had been speaking to Shallum in his position as keeper of the wardrobe. He had asked Shallum whether there were any collections of clothes that could be got rid of completely.

"Yes, my lord," replied Shallum promptly, "the special robes used for the worship of Baal and Asherah, not to mention the so-called queen of heaven. They can all be disposed of."

"Whose were those robes?" asked King Josiah, surprised. "I know that I have never worn them. In fact I don't think I have ever seen them."

"You have, my lord, you have," said Shallum with a wry smile. "Your father wore them often and they had a prominent position in his wardrobe. All of the larger garments were moved into storage when my lord became king. Then, by the time you were large enough to wear them, you had chosen to follow Yahweh, so these ones were never brought out."

"Let me see them," responded Josiah, obviously intrigued; "I want to see if I can recognise them."

Shallum said that they made their way to a back room that Josiah had apparently never even visited. Can you imagine having parts of your wardrobe that you have never visited? Apparently, once Shallum started to pull out the robes, Josiah did recognise some of them, although he had been very young when he had seen his father wearing them. They were highly decorated and looked more like a magician's clothes than anything else.

Shallum noticed that Josiah seemed to find them interesting and quite attractive, so when the king started to ask to see more, he said, "With all due respect, my lord, they are all rubbish and should be disposed of. May I do so?"

Quite a brave thing to say, when you think about it. Josiah had few things to remind him of his father, who had been assassinated as a young man – only twenty-four years old – when his son Josiah was eight. He had been an unpleasant man who enjoyed the trappings and comfort of royalty, revelling in the sensual opportunities provided by the worship of the many gods of his father. Late in life, his father Manasseh had chosen to repent and change his direction, but Amon was having none of that. Not for him the "restrictions" of Yahweh's laws; he wanted freedom, freedom to live a life of unrestrained selfishness and, when he could rouse himself from his idleness, dissipation. He relished opportunities to dress in opulent robes while worshipping various gods, and these were the robes that King Josiah was now spreading out on benches – running his hands over the exquisite materials and enjoying their softness. King Amon had liked to dress up in such clothes for special occasions, and had dressed the young Josiah in matching robes at times to present him to his gods and his people. He had not been unkind to the young boy Josiah, although who knows what he would have done if his misspent life had continued. The gods he worshipped were said to ask horrific and repugnant things of their adherents.

King Amon had exploited both men and women equally, and the outcry against him within the palace had grown quickly. It wasn't so much his religion that his servants found intolerable as his general attitude toward others, which was reflected in his religion. And it was obvious to all that he was getting worse as he exercised his power to indulge himself. Within two years, he had first alienated and then revolted enough of his servants that it was only a matter of time before someone took drastic action against him. The inevitable plot was successful, and that was the end of Amon. However, it was also the end of the plotters, as the populace wanted young Josiah to be king, not the rebellious servants.

Josiah had indeed become king, and had chosen to follow in the footsteps of his ancestor David and the worship of Yahweh, but now childhood memories of his father were stirring. These clothes the young child Josiah had admired and the grown-up Josiah still remembered.

He ran his hands over the robes, fingering their rich material and gaudy decoration, reliving past times with his father, and struggling with his conscience. He made no comment for several minutes, then finally asked Shallum, "Why are you so much against these clothes?"

Of course, Shallum was concerned that if they were kept, nostalgia and his few pleasant memories of his father might lead Josiah to take steps down a wrong path. He had resolutely avoided it so far, but many a man has been led astray by fine clothes and a yearning for comfort and popularity.

Shallum had responded simply, "Can you imagine what my wife would say if I didn't try to get rid of these?"

"Your wife?" asked King Josiah, absently. "Why?"

"Huldah, my wife, is a prophetess of Yahweh, my lord. God speaks to her from time to time. She couldn't be happy if you knowingly kept robes that had no other use than to indulge in idolatry. And nor could I, my lord," he finished.

Little more had been said on that occasion beyond Josiah agreeing that the robes should be thrown out and burned, but every so often after that, King Josiah had asked Shallum about Huldah and whether there were any messages from God. At times, there had been, and Josiah had found that Huldah's messages could be relied on – they were from God.

So when the Book of the Law was discovered and Josiah was eager to check if the scroll was genuine – whether the words that had been read from it were really the words of Yahweh – it was only natural for him to send his men to Huldah. "Not only that," he continued, "but even this morning he asked me whether there was any further information from God. It seems that he is a bit unsure as to what he should do with what he has learned from the Book of the Law."

CR

With perfect timing, Shallum came to the end of his story just as we arrived at his house. Stepping in through the doorway he called, "Shalom." I followed him through the doorway as a woman's voice answered, and then Huldah came from an inner room. When she saw me, her eyes lit up and a smile spread over her whole face. "Jeremiah, son of Hilkiah, it is good to see you back in Judah. I was talking to your father less than two weeks ago."

"It is good to be back, now that the Book of the Law of Yahweh has been found. Tell me what –" I started.

"Come and sit down," interrupted Shallum with a smile. "I think you are going to be talking for quite a long time, so why not sit down before you start?" He showed me to a seat next to the table that filled a significant part of the room. It was not a large room, nor was the house very big. The keeper of the king's wardrobe was obviously not a rich man. However, he did seem to be happy and

Huldah was the same. This small home had a feeling of peace that did not exist in my parents' much larger and more richly appointed house.

As soon as I could politely do so, I asked Huldah about her involvement with the Book of the Law and what she knew about it.

"It was just two weeks ago tomorrow that the word of Yahweh came to me," she answered. "He told me that on that day, that very day, the Book of the Law had been found.[18] Of course," she laughed, "I didn't know what the 'Book of the Law' actually was, so he had to explain to me that it was a book which Moses had written containing the laws God particularly wanted his nation to remember.[19] Apparently, it was to be kept with the ark of the covenant and read to the entire nation once every seven years when they were gathered for the Feast of Booths. It seems that the book was read to the entire nation after our people first conquered this land,[20] but I'm not sure whether the reading ever happened again. Obviously, sometime or other, it couldn't have been done, because the Book of the Law was separated from the ark of the covenant and the book was lost."

"So is that the book my father found?" I asked.

"Well, God told me that the book that was found was 'the Book of the Law'," she said doubtfully, "but I couldn't tell from his words whether it was the original written by Moses or a copy made later." Huldah spread out her

---

[18] We are not told how Huldah received the message from God which she delivered to Josiah's men. The events here are modelled loosely on God's ways of dealing with Ezekiel, who was told by God when important incidents had occurred or were about to occur in other places (e.g. Ezekiel 24:2, 27; 33:21-22).
[19] Deuteronomy 31:9-13, 24-29
[20] Joshua 8:30-35

hands in uncertainty. "Have you seen the scroll?" she asked. "Does it look old?"

I thought back to my view of the sheets, seen from a distance across the scroll room. "The scroll is obviously very old, but I have no idea whether it is *that* old. Why, the original scroll would be about eight or nine hundred years old!" I exclaimed. "Surely it couldn't be the original?"

"I don't know," Huldah mused. "If Yahweh wanted a scroll to last, it would, but he doesn't always work like that."

"No," I agreed. "It certainly looked old, what little I could see of it, but I don't know how we could tell if it was really that old. I wonder whether it had any markings on it indicating who wrote it out?"

"Shaphan might be the best person to ask," suggested Huldah. "He is an expert scribe and he has read the scroll at least three times now. He is sure to have looked for any sign of who wrote it. He probably couldn't help himself!" she concluded, smiling.

"Well, I certainly won't be asking Immer, if I can avoid it," I sighed.

"Immer would only want to know who the scribe was so that he could tell him off for any errors or badly shaped letters he found," laughed Shallum.

We all smiled as we thought of Immer telling off, well, possibly Moses! It didn't seem as absurd as it should have done.

Shallum was right, we did talk a lot, and I felt a kinship with this couple, she a prophetess and he a God-fearing Israelite. He was obviously proud of his wife's position as a messenger of God, but I had a feeling that he was a little too afraid of Yahweh to want any direct communication with him himself. God makes us all different and uses each of us differently. Shallum made it easy for Huldah to do her work for God. Huldah made it possible for Shallum to come closer to God than he would ever have dared by himself.

As Huldah continued to explain the events of those days, she was also able to tell me some of the contents of the Book of the Law. God had told her that King Josiah would send a delegation to seek Yahweh's guidance for the king and the nation, because of the curses heard from the Book of the Law. God had given her the answer to report to the king, but had also told her what the curses were which had so worried Josiah.

The curses were, quite frankly, terrifying. Yahweh had always been presented to me by my parents as the God who was on Israel's side, but that did not seem to match God's opinion. God's opinion was that Israel had to be on his side, and that if they were, blessings without number would be poured upon the nation. However, if Israel followed any other god, or walked away from God to choose their own paths, unimaginable terrors would result.

My nation pictured Yahweh as a nagging but doting grandfather who would pester them for obedience, but would, when the final decisions had to be made, be loyal to them and support them. The Book of the Law painted a different picture, one of a God who would visit horrifying curses upon a nation that was unfaithful.

One of the curses which Huldah could repeat to me went like this:

> "Because you did not serve the Lord your God
> with joyfulness and gladness of heart,
> because of the abundance of all things,
> therefore you shall serve your enemies
> whom the Lord will send against you,
> in hunger and thirst, in nakedness,

and lacking everything.
And he will put a yoke of iron on your neck
until he has destroyed you.
The Lord will bring a nation against you
from far away, from the end of the earth,
swooping down like the eagle,
a nation whose language you do not understand,
a hard-faced nation who shall not respect the old
or show mercy to the young."[21]

What a stark choice was presented, and it was one my nation had already made. We had not served Yahweh with joy and gladness, but instead had complained that he was a god who unfairly limited our freedom. Our search for joy and gladness had taken us to the altars of idols instead. And how closely this description fitted with God's words to me about the coming destruction of Judah through the attacks of nations from afar!

In the future, I would also see more meaning in the reference to a yoke of iron and many of the other details, but that was to unfold later. For now, it was just a frightening snippet of a future my nation would not even contemplate.

King Josiah's godly fear had been roused by these curses. Shaphan had explained to Huldah that the king had felt responsible for the godless behaviour of the nation. Not only that, but as the current king, he also felt responsibility for the ways of his ancestors who had not led the people towards God. These responsibilities he felt so keenly that he could not face a representative of God, but sent a delegation instead.

Huldah was pleased to explain how God had promised Josiah a peaceful life because of his humble attitude. This was good news in my ears and gave some

---

[21] Deuteronomy 28:47-50

form of answer to the question that had bothered me: "When will God's judgement come?" The answer must be that it would come sometime after Josiah's death. There would be at least one more king of Judah after Josiah. One other thing had bothered me about my father's attitude, so I asked Huldah, "You said that Josiah's attitude was very humble. What about the attitude of the delegation he sent?"

"Ah," she said, "that was not so humble. There was nothing rude or overbearing, but none came with an attitude like the one that kept Josiah away. None of them came as if overwhelmed by the magnitude of Judah's sin."

"Why should they be so concerned?" asked Shallum. "They are not evil men who have ignored God's commands."

"You are right," agreed Huldah, "but have they always tried to lead the people in the ways of God as described in the Book of the Law?"

"No, I suppose they haven't," mused her husband. "Josiah has done much more. Each of them has tried to resist some of Josiah's reforms – the reforms God has considered so necessary. Yet Josiah feels his guilt much more sharply."

"Yes, we are blessed to have Josiah as king, and not one of the others," I observed. "Otherwise, the kingdom might have been destroyed already."

"I suppose you could be right," said Huldah. "I hadn't thought of it that way."

"Can we do anything to help King Josiah and our nation?" asked Shallum.

We discussed this question and shared our thoughts together. Were there any ways we could contribute? Huldah had already delivered God's message to the king. What would be the effects of the message? Although not quite as immediate as the threat delivered by Jonah, the promise of destruction was just as comprehensive, and the message deserved the same response. Should we leave it entirely up to King Josiah to provide that response, or could we help?

Suddenly it came to me: the Book of the Law, that was the answer. Huldah had mentioned that the Book of the Law was meant to be read to the people every seven years during the Feast of Tabernacles, in the seventh month. We had missed the right time because the eighth month had already begun, but why not do it anyway? Why not gather all the people together and read them the Book of the Law?

Chapter 6

Meeting Josiah

The shadows cast by the guardhouse had changed to the other side during my absence. By the time I returned to the gates of King Josiah's palace, it was mid-afternoon, and the question on my mind was, how could I get in to see the king?

Shaphan might be my best possibility, though of course, I didn't know whether or not he would be in the palace at this time of day. Asking the guard who had helped me in the morning, I found that, yes, Shaphan was in the palace.

"Could I speak with him?" I asked.

The guard looked at me doubtfully. "I'm not sure," he answered. "I can try to find him, but the palace is a busy place at the moment, what with that discovery in the temple. Everyone is wondering what to do – though I can't see what there is to get excited about myself," he said, confidingly. "We got by without it for however long – but then again, I'm only a guard."

He told his three fellow guards where he was going and marched off towards the front entrance of the main palace building. He climbed the stairs and disappeared inside. I moved into the small area of shade provided by the gatepost. It seemed likely that my wait would last some time, so I might as well get as comfortable as possible.

However, while I waited, a squad of soldiers suddenly came marching down the steps at the front of the palace towards me, and shortly afterwards a small group of men followed them down the steps. They were deep in conversation, but I recognised King Josiah in the middle. Shaphan too was there, along with several others of the group of nobles whom I had dubbed the "six mysterious men" when they had come several times to listen to the words of Yahweh at the start of my work of prophesying. The king and his entourage swept towards me and I had little time to think.

"My lord, O king," I called, and stepped forward.

The closest man turned and surveyed me. "You!" he said with a contemptuous curl of his lip. It was Asaiah, the king's young friend who had so aggressively criticised the words of God in my mouth. "I thought you had taken your carping criticism to other countries," he sneered.

It seemed that time had not softened his opinion of me. I ignored him.

"My lord, O king!" I repeated, louder this time, and King Josiah turned towards me.

"Jeremiah, the son of Hilkiah!" he exclaimed. "I was advised that you were in Rabbah. A speedy return? or has someone been hiding things from me again?" As he spoke this last sentence, he turned and smiled meaningfully at the man on his right. Shaphan the secretary returned his smile and even looked a little pleased to see me. We had got to know each other during the tour of Israel in Josiah's thirteenth year as king. Our relationship had got off to a poor start in Jerusalem when Shaphan had tried to hide God's message from Josiah and I had sidestepped him and spoken to the king directly. However, his support of King Josiah over the intervening years and his willingness to allow the young king to choose his own path in life and to rule the kingdom as he saw fit were a testament to his faithful character.

"I had to return when I heard the news about the Book of the Law," I replied.

"We are just going to the scroll room in the temple now," said Josiah. "Come with us. I have some questions to ask you."

This was an honour indeed: to be invited by the king to inspect his most important project. I tried to keep my ego under control, but it was hard not to feel a little distinguished as I walked to the temple with the group of nobles. True, I was not the one talking to the king, but I was one of only a few walking with him, and I was the one he wanted to ask questions of. Pride is such a deceptive and foolish thing. My pride tells me that I, Jeremiah, am important, but in what way was it me who was important? Josiah only wanted to hear from me because he wanted to hear words from God. And why did I have words from God to pass on? Because God had chosen me even before I was born. Everything that could possibly give me status had come from God. A very obvious fact, but despite this, I walked along in a haze of pride, hoping that some of my relatives or friends would notice me.

Thankfully, no-one did, or it might have become even more of a problem for me. Instead, we walked the short distance to the temple almost without seeing anyone. We entered the temple through the new gate and walked directly to the scroll room.

As we entered, the room looked much the same as it had in the morning, except that my father was now sitting at another table near the centre of the room, reading a sheet of parchment. He had the look of one who is having to concentrate very hard on what he is reading, moving his head up and down to find the position in which the letters looked clearest. Immer was still seated on the platform and the hapless scribe in the corner was looking more downcast than ever. Maybe he *had* made another mistake just before I left.

"Greetings, Immer," said King Josiah.

"Peace, my lord the king," responded Immer.

"What progress do you have to report?" asked the king.

"This is a difficult work, my lord, but progress is good. The sixteen scribes producing the copies are now waiting for the checking to finish so that they can start the copying of a second sheet," Immer advised. "Ah – all, that is, except one."

Immer had a very good sideways look – practiced over many years – that apportioned blame without him needing to speak, and he put it to good use here. All who had been in his classes had seen and felt that glance, and now the scribe in the corner quailed under it, but kept his eyes glued on the piece of parchment his pen was carefully ornamenting. King Josiah followed Immer's glance and looked as if he was about to ask a question, but Immer continued: "The first copy of each of the sixteen sheets has been initially checked by myself and also by one other scribe, while the third check of each is in progress. As expected, no further errors have been found, and the remaining eight checks will be undertaken over the next two days. Those undertaken tomorrow will follow the same procedure, while any remaining on the last day will be slightly less rigorous, but will also undertake some different sorts of checks, counting the numbers of characters in lines and such like, where our updating and modernising of the script has not made such tests impossible for this first copy."

King Josiah looked interested in this last comment. "You mean that all of the copying has been done using the same line divisions, columns and so on?" he asked.

"Yes, where possible," replied Immer. "It makes it easier to check in many ways."

"That makes good sense," said Josiah, and looked around the room again. He noticed my father this time and asked, "Hilkiah, are you happy with the progress of the work?"

Technically at least, my father was in overall charge of this entire operation. One of the instructions included in the Book of the Law was that it was to be cared for by the priests, so as High Priest, my father had final responsibility for and control over this scroll and its reproduction.

"Yes," he replied in that delightfully deep voice, "the work proceeds well, with only one sheet requiring rewriting. A trifling error, really – just a repeated word – but it cannot be repaired invisibly, so a new sheet is being prepared. This has required some minor adjustments to the plan, but nothing significant. The scribe who made the mistake is quite young, and will work some extra hours to catch up again."

"So completion of my copy is still on target?" asked Josiah.

"Yes," interrupted Immer; "although much may still change before everything is complete, you can still expect your personal copy in about 40 days. A very quick job, if I may say so."

"And yet it also seems a long time," Josiah mused. "The curses in the Book of the Law are so terrible. Urgent action is required. Judah must start to follow the commands in the Book of the Law. What can we do?"

Now seemed to be the time to put forward my suggestion about reading the Book of the Law, but something made me wait.

Shaphan agreed that the matter was urgent and suggested calling all of the leaders together. Leaders and elders from all of the tribes and towns – they were the ones who would be able to understand the message and make sure the people obeyed.

All of the nobles supported the proposal and Josiah looked pleased that at least something could be done immediately. "An excellent suggestion," he agreed. "Shaphan, write letters in my name commanding that all leaders and elders from every town come to me in Jerusalem."

"Yes, my lord," said Shaphan. "When must they arrive?"

"How soon is it possible to send around the message that demands their attendance?" the king asked. "Today is the third day of the new moon."

"Such a thing hasn't been done for some time, my lord," said Shaphan, "but if we are working with the utmost urgency, we could set a date of seven days from tomorrow[22]. That takes us to the eleventh day of the eighth month." He looked thoughtful. "I can go and write the letter now if you will check it this evening, my lord," he offered. "Tomorrow we can make the copies we need and send out the messengers to the most distant places first."

---

[22] An example with only 3 days' notice is given in Ezra 10:7-8

"Very good," said Josiah with a smile. "Go and start now. When I finish here, I will come and see you."

Shaphan left the room and everyone present looked a little dumbfounded, except for Josiah. Everyone had known that Josiah thought this important, but this was a bold, sweeping demand for action, rather than the more considered, limited announcements that were typical of leaders. Josiah simply looked pleased.

The discussion returned to the copying process. Since this had been a day of checking, no new work had been done except for the single replacement sheet that was being made. Josiah took the opportunity to walk around the room reading sections from each of the sheets as they were being checked. One of these sheets would form part of his own copy of the Book of the Law, although it had not yet been decided which one. That would depend on which scribe could produce the flawless copy required over the entire sixteen sheets of the Book of the Law while also achieving the most beautiful result. About 23,000 words would have to be copied so that they were easy to read, attractively presented and completely without errors. *Any* errors. It would be a major achievement for a scribe to have his work selected for presentation to the king, and would reflect remarkable skill in his profession. Josiah, however, was more interested in the words of the Book of the Law than its presentation. He scanned the sheets as he moved around the room, and read out sections that caught his attention.

At one table, he scanned the sheet for a few seconds and then looked up and beckoned to me. "Jeremiah," he called, "look at this." I hurried across eagerly. Here was my opportunity to read some of the Book of the Law!

"Look at this passage, Jeremiah:

" 'All these curses shall come upon you
and pursue you and overtake you

till you are destroyed, because you did not obey
the voice of the Lord your God,
to keep his commandments and his statutes
that he commanded you.'[23] ”

Josiah read fluently from the newly copied sheet, written in our modern script using all of the improved writing conventions which make it so much easier for laypeople to read.

“Jeremiah, these are the words that made me so fearful,” Josiah said earnestly. He stood up and looked at me as he continued, “Yahweh our God has made these threats and he has the power to carry them out. One of the questions I want to ask you is when this will happen – and why hasn’t it happened already?” His finger hovered over the passage and he hurried on without waiting for an answer to his question, “God’s words continue:

“ ‘Because you did not serve the Lord your God
with joyfulness and gladness of heart,
because of the abundance of all things,
therefore you shall serve your enemies
whom the Lord will send against you,
in hunger and thirst, in nakedness,
and lacking everything.
And he will put a yoke of iron on your neck
until he has destroyed you.
The Lord will bring a nation against you
from far away, from the end of the earth,
swooping down like the eagle,
a nation whose language you do not understand,
a hard-faced nation who shall not respect the old
or show mercy to the young.'[24] ”

---

[23] Deuteronomy 28:45
[24] Deuteronomy 28:47-50

Josiah stopped reading, looked at me seriously and said, "Those words were so similar to some of your words that I was utterly convinced and completely terrified." King Josiah smiled a little awkwardly as he remembered his feelings on that afternoon, the deep shame that had caused him to tear his robe and weep for his kingdom as he understood for the first time how God really felt about Israel and Judah. "I don't feel so terrified of immediate punishment since Huldah pronounced God's merciful response, but I still feel very responsible for our failure to obey God until now. I have been king for more than seventeen years and still the land is full of idols. My nation still has very little knowledge of God. Not even fifty people in Judah have read the Book of the Law of Yahweh who led us into this land."

"My lord Josiah, Huldah the prophetess mentioned the same passage to me, so I have had some time to think about it," I began, then continued a little more tentatively. "During the time of your ancestor Uzziah, Isaiah the son of Amoz was told he should continue to prophesy until the cities lay desolate[25]. Isaiah died and so did your fathers, yet the cities of Judah still do not lie desolate. Why? Probably because some of your ancestors listened to God's words and did their best to change our nation. Unfortunately, at different times, other kings have also changed the nation for the worse: Ahaz, Manasseh, and even your own father."

Josiah looked at me seriously again, and this time there was also a tinge of sadness in his eyes. "Who will win, Jeremiah? Yahweh's servants or his enemies? It seems that every time a king tries to direct his people back to God, the next king comes along and reverses all of his good work."

---

[25] Isaiah 6:11

"You are right, O king," I responded. "That must be why God continues to renew his warnings through prophets like Isaiah. But the warnings in the Book of the Law show that these warnings and curses will be fulfilled when our God decides that the sin of our nation is too great to be redeemed."

"And when will that be?" King Josiah asked.

"You are probably helping to decide the answer to that question now," I guessed.

"Listen to this passage too, Jeremiah," said Josiah as he leaned over the sheet of parchment again:

" 'They shall besiege you in all your towns,
until your high and fortified walls, in which you trusted,
come down throughout all your land.
And they shall besiege you
in all your towns throughout all your land,
which the Lord your God has given you.'[26]

"These words are so similar to some of your words when you talked about enemies coming from the north, but I can't remember the exact wording. Can you?"

The king had put me on the spot and it was surprising how difficult it was to stop and identify the words he had referred to so that I could repeat them for him. Not only could I read them in my mind at any time, but I knew them all off by heart – I had delivered them hundreds of times over that three-month period when God had said that I must "speak to Jerusalem". After a few seconds I managed to identify the section he was referring to and repeated it to him:

" 'For behold, I am calling all the tribes
of the kingdoms of the north, declares the Lord,
and they shall come, and every one shall set his throne

---

[26] Deuteronomy 28:52

> at the entrance of the gates of Jerusalem,
> against all its walls all around
> and against all the cities of Judah.'[27]"

Josiah's eyes remained glued to mine as I recited these words, and when I had finished he drew a deep breath.

"I was right," he said, and sighed. "Your words are very similar, and when I take them in conjunction with the words of God through Huldah, I am convinced that they will be fulfilled eventually, whatever I may try to do. Not in my lifetime, thanks to God's mercy, but maybe within only five or six generations after that."

His words struck a chord with me, so that I remember them as if they had been said only yesterday. They seemed completely convincing, but so pessimistic. Surely we could do something to avert the disaster?

History has shown that Josiah's words were in fact far too *optimistic*. Instead of judgement coming within five or six generations, Jerusalem was destroyed during the very next generation. Josiah's own sons were to sign the nation's death warrant, and all of Josiah's good work would be undone by three worthless sons and a worthless grandson.

Ignorance of the future can be such a blessing.

CR

Josiah spent a full hour in the scroll room that day. An hour taken from his busy schedule and offered as a sacrifice to Yahweh. Probably some special interest group had been refused an audience with the king so that he could pursue his religion. His nobles saw it and took note, and so did the nation's top scribes. Even the High Priest saw the king's dedication and felt a little guilty – as he told

---

[27] Jeremiah 1:15

me humbly while we walked back to Anathoth in the dying light of the setting sun.

A change *was* coming to the nation. I could feel it in the atmosphere of the scroll room, and I could see it in the looks exchanged between the leaders of the country. Authentic commitment is hard to resist, and there was no doubt about their young king's commitment to Yahweh.

Like ripples on a pond, King Josiah's enthusiasm was spreading outwards to others. Change was coming, but would it be enough?

Chapter 7

Unpleasant surprises

They were waiting for me as we walked along the path on the outskirts of Anathoth: a welcoming committee, standing discontented in the gathering night. There was no time spent in niceties or polite enquiries about my health, just an angry question from the closest agitator: "How dare you touch our god?"

Before I could answer, another of the group continued with a very thinly veiled warning: "Sometimes only a blood sacrifice can atone for such an insult, you know. Nothing less could be sure to mollify our powerful god."

Apparently someone from Anathoth had seen enough of my attack on their erstwhile deity to walk around and investigate. Having found the object of their devotion lying in small fragments along the path, the straw from inside wafting around in the gentle breeze, the loyal subject had returned and spent the remainder of the day discussing my heinous crime with other like-minded idolaters. When they had garnered enough moral support, and strengthened it through an afternoon spent with a skin of wine, eight of them had assembled outside the town to wait for my return, and they were not going to let their ire cool. It is easy to be a little flippant looking back because I know that I survived the exchange, but at the time, I wasn't so sure that I would.

"He deserves to die!" shouted one of the group, raising a cudgel above his head. The heavy, gnarled branch had initially been hidden behind him, but now it was in clear view and his intention was just as clear.

I stepped forward, reached up and grabbed the hand holding the cudgel, and my assailant and I struggled for control of it. However, wine had dulled my opponent's senses, and it was not long before I had the weapon and he was cowering away from me. A noise from behind warned me that another attack was coming, and two quick steps forward caused the hastily aimed fist to miss me. This man too was feeling the effects of the wine with which he had whiled away the afternoon. When his swinging fist met no resistance, he stumbled forward, tripped in the gloom and landed prone at my feet. No-one else had interfered while the fracas lasted, and once it was over there was less enthusiasm for attacking me. Was this just good fortune, or yet another fulfilment of the promise to protect me as long as I would not cringe before my opponents?

Throughout this short but terrifying exchange, my father had stood mute and motionless, leaving me to fend for myself. The humble guilt confessed on the journey home had not lasted long, nor had it inspired either word or action.

Thankfully, God had not abandoned me.

It was quite some time before we could continue our journey home. Although no-one else attacked me physically, the trouble was not yet over. The eight men were all agreed that the destruction of their idol was a major crime requiring retribution. Since they had failed in their attempt to punish me privately, they would take it up with the other town leaders. They assured me that I had not heard the last of it. There were even veiled threats of midnight attacks and possible damage to our house. That was when my father finally got involved and advised them not to do anything like that if they valued their own property. I recognised some of the men, but my father referred to them all by name as the confrontation wound down. One was Kish, the father of my childhood friend Benaiah.

Throughout the discussion, there was no suggestion that the offended god might take his own steps to punish me, nor was there any suggestion from the High Priest that their god was an abomination that demanded action, or that I had been right in what I did.

Stony silence formed a wall between my father and me as we walked the short distance home. I asked if he knew what would happen next, but his only answer was a gruff, "We shall see," and after that, silence.

Our arrival home would have been just like old times, except for the hostility I felt from my father. Cooking smells wafted along the path and a warm light crept through the cracks in the shutters and under the door.

I pushed the door open and stepped back to let my father enter. For the first time since the confrontation on the outskirts of Anathoth, I could see his face, and I was surprised to see the anger that smouldered there. His jaw was tightly clenched and the look in his eyes as he walked past me didn't bode well for my peace of mind.

My mother noticed his manner immediately and looked questioningly at me as I followed him through the doorway. Closing the door behind me, I told her about the idol we had seen in the grove that morning. As I recounted my actions, my father pursed and un-pursed his lips and nearly interrupted more than once. His obvious fury was puzzling me a little, and finally I interrupted my story and asked, "Why are you so angry, father?"

Two servants were in the room arranging items on the table in preparation for our meal. Our parents' rules for the house had always forbidden arguing or any display of anger in front of the servants, but it seemed clear to me that this rule was to be sorely tested tonight.

"Your behaviour was utterly unacceptable, Jeremiah," he said, and his voice had none of the mellifluous beauty with which he commonly spoke. Instead, it was harsh, and the words had a cutting edge. "This town has had peace since the days of King Solomon, yet when you return from your gallivanting around the world, you have us at each other's throats within a day!" He turned and walked to the other end of the room, obviously striving for control. It evaded him and he turned back to me, "It is foolishness to look for fights. And even greater foolishness to attack a man in such a position as Benaiah, the son of Kenan."

"Which one was Benaiah?" I asked.

"Benaiah was the one you attacked. He is more than twice your age and one of the chief men of Anathoth! And he is one of the men who cares for the idol you demolished in your foolishness."

The word "foolishness" was obviously a mainstay of my father's vocabulary that night. It upset me at the time, but I was also struck forcibly by the irony of my father's words when taken with the words of King David:

"The fool says in his heart, 'There is no God.'
They are corrupt, they do abominable deeds,
there is none who does good."[28]

David ascribed foolishness to those who denied the God of Israel, but I was being attacked for foolishness because I had acknowledged him as the only God of Israel.

The servants had stopped their work and were watching open-mouthed. My father was widely known for his measured approach to life and his willingness to build cooperation with all; yet here he was, attacking his own son! It was certainly not ordinary behaviour from my father, but I noticed that one of the servants was looking rather pleased. I couldn't understand the servant's attitude at the time, and felt rather overwhelmed.

My mother had moved quietly across the room and rested her hand on my father's arm. The unspoken warning was obvious. Once again my father struggled to regain control of himself, and this time he succeeded.

"We will say no more about this," he said in a voice much more like his ordinary voice, and the servants quickly got back to work. "But don't be surprised when there is trouble in the morning," he concluded.

Our evening meal began soon after that and my father said very little during it. Meanwhile, I was trying to decide when to raise the question of the women in the temple, a decision which had not been made any easier by the ongoing confrontation over my assault on an idolater's useless handiwork. In my opinion, this matter was serious, and I certainly did not want to raise the question in front of the servants. I would have preferred to have discussed it on the way home, but my father had wanted to discuss more about the schedule for copying the Book of the Law.

---

[28] Psalm 14:1; Psalm 53:1

This was quite a fiddly process because the sheets being copied or checked could only be used effectively by one person at a time. Scheduling all of the copying and checking to take this into account required careful thought, and my father was not confident that all of the possibilities had been considered. So we had talked about scheduling and organisation instead of content. It was frustrating, but probably necessary.

Finally the meal was over and we had some time during which the servants would be eating their own meals and then cleaning up. My mother needed to do a little work on some new sleeping mats for winter. Most of the work had been done by the servants, but my mother always liked to do the final touches herself. This took her out of the room, and for once I was glad. I was not looking forward to this discussion.

As soon as my mother had left the room, I turned to my father, but he was already speaking to me, intent on continuing the discussion limited by the presence of the servants.

"Jeremiah, I don't know quite how to say this, but your behaviour must change," he began. "Ever since you started to act like a prophet, you have caused trouble and division everywhere. You are concentrating on yourself and nobody else. Even events as important as your brothers' weddings were not important enough for you to attend. And what have you achieved? Nothing except to upset everyone."

This was a completely unexpected attack, and I had no idea how to respond. I had believed that my father had understood my absence for Azariah's wedding and my sadness at missing Gemariah's wedding, but clearly he had not. The burden of my work for Yahweh felt even heavier and for a time I felt overwhelmed and exhausted. Would anyone ever understand?

It took quite some time to explain, yet again, the circumstances of my call as a prophet to the nations and the frequent instructions from God that took me to other lands. Self-justification is almost irresistible, but rarely achieves the desired aim. My father's opinion was immovable and the set of his mouth made it clear that he found my protestations unconvincing.

"That's all finished now," said my mother happily, re-entering the room during a lull in our disjointed conversation. "It's good to get the work for winter finished before the cold weather begins."

She looked from my father to me and the strain between us must have been visible to her. But it wasn't the way of our family to be open in such matters. Appearances must be maintained and conflicts were normally papered over and left to fester until they finally had to be resolved or simply died a natural death. My father's behaviour today had been very unusual, showing just how important he considered these matters.

So now my opportunity was gone and the question must be asked in front of my mother. My father obviously did not intend to continue our argument in front of her, so instead I must introduce another subject which seemed likely to cause even more hurt.

"Father," I said, and he looked at me with warning in his eyes, not wanting me to continue the previous subject. In the event, he probably would have been happier if I had continued that subject, but instead, I began to describe what had happened in the temple area after I had left the scroll room that morning. As I described the building with the door left ajar, my father stiffened and started to look a little edgy. Describing the room and its inhabitants was rather difficult because I didn't want to describe the pictures at all, but there was little to get upset about without this context. However, my father clearly didn't want all of the details either, and that removed the last of my doubts. My father knew that room. He knew the women and their work.

Suddenly I did want to describe the work of these women and to force my father to acknowledge that he, the High Priest of Yahweh, allowed work for the worship of Baal to continue unhindered in Yahweh's temple. What could make him do such a thing? I knew that he believed in Yahweh in his own way, and worshipped him, so how could this possibly happen?

But still, my mother…? A while later, I had much of the information I had wanted and was fairly sure of the rest, even though it had all been discussed guardedly, as both my father and I wanted to protect my mother as much as possible – although probably for quite different reasons.

"So do you receive money from these women or their masters for the use of rooms in God's temple?" I asked, wanting to confirm the few details which had not yet been clarified.

"That is nothing to do with this discussion, nor is it any of your business," snapped my father.

Again, I suspected that this meant that the answer was yes, but I still wanted confirmation if possible.

"Father, it is up to you to decide whether or not to answer this question, but for me it is very much part of the subject we are discussing. I have appreciated your care for me throughout my life, but if the food at your table is provided by worshippers of Baal, paid by them to allow them to help others to worship Baal, then I cannot eat it."

"Oh, Jeremiah," my mother breathed, afraid of where this might lead.

"Jeremiah," my father replied, appearing to be caught between irritation and concern, "you continue to create conflict where it doesn't need to exist. You don't need to worry about these women or their work. They are not trying to convince you to worship Baal, and what they do for themselves need not concern you."

Not trying to convince me? Incredulously, I thought back to the behaviour of the woman I had run away from, and there was no question that her intent had *not* been to leave me alone! But I did not just want these women to limit what they did – I wanted them out of the temple forever.

"You have read the words of God speaking against idols," I urged. "Surely you know that the worship of idols in this land can never be acceptable? You have read the Psalms and Isaiah, and must surely understand that idol worship makes our land repulsive to God? It doesn't matter whether the worshippers try to convince us or not, they cannot be allowed to remain, let alone be given a home in the house of God. This is what God said to Isaiah:

> " 'shall I not do to Jerusalem and her idols
> as I have done to Samaria and her images?'[29]"

"Yahweh wants our worship," my father argued. "He wants us to acknowledge him and worship him in his temple, but the survival of our worship has often depended on patience and tolerance when less dedicated kings have been in charge. Even King Josiah allows this spirit of cooperation to continue."

"Does he approve of these women and their work?" I asked, shocked.

"None of this is done in secret," my father replied. "The chariots of the sun, the altars to Baal and so on, these are all obvious in the temple area and are major reasons why the worship of Yahweh has survived at all in

---

[29] Isaiah 10:11

Judah. Tolerance and cooperation are victories of good sense that you should learn, my son. Now let us have no more of this divisive discussion. You have upset your mother and what have you achieved? No more, Jeremiah."

There seemed to be no real choice, so the discussion stopped. Soon afterwards, I left the room and went to my own room. A room of my own – another benefit of the riches I was now questioning.

CR

In my room that night, I spent an hour reading from the smelly scroll of Isaiah which I now possessed as my own, a gift from my father after a new copy had been made. He would have preferred to have given me a new copy, but I was attached to this scroll which had done so much to teach me about the ways of God. Even the smallest hint of its stale, musty smell recalled many passages of Isaiah to my mind, and I would have been very sorry to part with it. A lamp illuminated the bench as I unrolled the scroll and reminded myself of God's words against idolatry. Could God's utter condemnation of any worship compromised by idol worship possibly fit with my father's oft-repeated mantra of "tolerance and cooperation"?

I was having to face the same fight within myself too. If I made a stand against my father's attitudes, I would surely be looking for a new place to stay, and how would I finance that? Much of the money I had used as a prophet to the nations had been supplied by my father. Could I continue in this way now that I knew – or thought I knew – where at least some of that money came from?

This day had delivered shock after shock, and now I must end it with thoughts of leaving home permanently, with no further access to my family's wealth.

That night, I spent several hours in prayer as the knowledge sank in that my life had been turned upside down again. No longer could I stay in rich comfort eating food paid for by the earnings of women who wove hangings for Baal and Asherah in the temple of Yahweh.

Fitful sleep followed before I woke in the grey of early dawn and dragged myself wearily from my bed. Another day meant more decisions, and I had always found it easier when I had confirmed my decisions from earlier days before the next wave of difficulties struck.

I had left it too late.

Chapter 8

Friends

Arriving at my favourite place of meditation that morning, I met another surprise. My childhood friend Benaiah was sitting on my preferred pile of rocks, waiting for me.

"This is a surprise, Benaiah," I said. We had been good friends when we were younger, but he had never shown any strong desire to move closer to God. This had caused us to grow apart since God had called me to work as a prophet.

"Don't you know what I am here for?" he asked, and his angry tone surprised me.

"No, I have no idea," I replied, doubtfully.

"I thought you were a prophet," he sneered, "able to tell the future – supposedly – and yet you don't even know a simple thing like that. Pretty pathetic, if you ask me." He stood and took a step towards me, "You're in deep trouble, you are. And I think you deserve to be," he finished, and there was a bitterness in his voice that he had never used with me before.

"Why?" I asked, cautiously, starting to guess what this was all about.

"My uncle, Benaiah the son of Kenan, the one I am named after, is going to do his best to get you beaten for breaking up our image," he explained. "And I also heard that you attacked him last night."

"Me – attack him?" I asked incredulously. "I did defend myself from him when he threatened me with a heavy stick, but no, I did not attack him."

"That's not the way my father told the story," Benaiah replied, doubtfully, "and he was there."

"So was I, you know," I said drily, but I could feel the anger building in me and it was hard to keep my voice steady.

"Well, I wish you hadn't started all the trouble in the first place," said Benaiah. "It was stupid of you."

"And I wish you would stop supporting a dead idol – a lump of plaster, straw and paint," I said angrily. "Think about what your name means, Benaiah. 'Yahweh delivers'[30] is a good name to have, but he won't deliver you when you worship other gods."

"You and I have been good friends, Jeremiah, but you've never behaved like this before," Benaiah snapped. "Why did you do it? You can't demolish our shrine, ruin our god and attack a leading man of the village, and expect to just get away with it."

"And you can't expect to worship other gods without making the true, living God angry," I answered, now controlling my anger and speaking more calmly. "A

---

[30] There are several opinions about what the name Benaiah means, but this is one of the most popular.

nation from the north is coming to destroy our nation because of exactly this sort of behaviour!"

"So you're so much better than everybody else, aren't you!" Benaiah sneered. "I thought my uncle was overdoing it in wanting to have you beaten, but now I'm starting to hope he succeeds."

There was nothing more to be said, really, but we argued for a while anyway. We had reached a decisive parting of the ways, Benaiah and I, and he was now just one more opponent to add to my ever-growing list.

∞

Benaiah left without saying goodbye, and I knew that my words would be passed on to his father and uncle before very long. What should I do? To stay in Anathoth and see what happened with the so-called charges would mean a delay in telling King Josiah about the women in the temple and about my suggestion of reading the book of the law to the people. But on the other hand, to be absent during the presentation of such charges before the judges would be to lay myself open to all sorts of false claims and unjust punishment. It was possible that it would all blow over; that the cold light of day would cause my antagonists to re-consider their course.

But what if it didn't blow over? What if I found a group of the judges' men waiting for me this evening, ready to give me forty stripes?

Everything seemed to be getting out of control!

Immer had attacked me again. That was no surprise – he attacked everyone – but it had been another unpleasant experience.

Twice, now, my father had not supported or defended me when men had threatened to beat me up.

Women were weaving hangings for Baal and Asherah in the temple. My father knew it and probably even collected income from it.

Some of the leading men of Anathoth were planning to bring charges against me for destroying an idol which should never have been allowed in the land at all. Even my friend hoped they would succeed in their attempts to get me beaten for it.

I sat down on the pile of stones and thought. A prophet to the nations? I had found that to be much safer than being a prophet to Judah, but I had to do both. Not only that, but God would not let me run away. Last night I had almost decided that I needed to leave my home and live somewhere else. I had considered moving to Jerusalem, but with this threat of legal attacks on me, would this be running away – the running away that God had forbidden me to do?

What to do? What did I want to do?

It seemed less important, but I also had the problem of family: when could I visit Azariah and Gemariah and their families? Already, I had delayed longer than I wanted to, and any more delay would only spark more criticism.

And what about the Book of the Law? I must read it, but how?

The stress was beginning to tell. After Benaiah left me that morning, I could hardly meditate at all. Instead, I sat on that pile of stones and my review of events became a catalogue of woes, and my prayers and praise to God never happened at all.

ಌ

There was a frosty atmosphere in our house as we ate the morning meal. My mother did not want to talk about the subject of last night lest more trouble arise, and my father did not want to talk to me at all, so the meal was eaten in silence. Gone was the enthusiasm of the previous morning and the welcome of the night before that. I was a lead weight in the house, and I'm sure my father would have paid quite a lot of his beloved money to have had me far away, back in Rabbah of the Ammonites, or even further afield. It is not a pleasant feeling to know that you are not wanted in your parents' home.

℘

After the meal, I went to visit Chelub, another close childhood friend. The visit was short and the welcome there was cold also. Benaiah was a shared friend, and he had already visited Chelub earlier in the morning to recount my crimes. It seemed that I was now a shared enemy and that the loving God of Israel was hated too.

I left, wondering how things could have come to such a pass in Judah – and that in a town of priests! King Josiah wanted to serve Yahweh, but his nation would not. The king destroyed false idols, and his people simply built new ones and hid them from the king under every green tree.

Chelub had also said that he was hoping I would be punished because that would help to cool the ideas of reform that were rising in the hearts of some people. He hoped I would be made an example of.

Friends!

℘

Back in our home, I found my mother giving the day's instructions to the servants. My father had already left for Jerusalem and planned to stay there overnight. Apparently there were some problems with the copying of the Book of the Law which had not been mentioned to

King Josiah, and my father and Immer were hoping to sort them out without needing to inform the king. Clearly, I was not a part of his plans for the day.

My mother waited until the most pressing work with the servants was complete and then turned to me.

"Can we talk, Jeremiah?" she asked.

"If you have the time, Mother, I would really appreciate it," I replied.

One of the problems with having servants is that they are always around. Our house was large, but not enormous, and the servants' work of preparing for winter would take them into all of the rooms. My mother had firm ideas about preparations for winter – every room must be cleaned and checked before the wind and rain of winter tested every shutter and exploited every crack. Where could we talk in private? The words I needed to speak would criticise many arrangements and the people behind them.

My mother looked at me briefly and understood without me needing to explain. "Delaiah," she called to our household manager, "leave the work in the scroll room until the afternoon."

We went into the scroll room and, as I closed the door, my mother asked, "Are you really thinking that you cannot stay in our house, Jeremiah? Your suggestion hurt your father deeply, you know."

Her words were a shock, but as I considered it, they made sense. My father's objections to me were based on my behaviour. If I would just cooperate with his ideas and desires, I would be very welcome in his house. Already I had learned that most people who objected to my words or actions did so simply because they did not fit in with the norms of society. Few people seem to have genuine religious commitments themselves – they simply follow the crowd. If the crowd can be convinced to do right, most will follow, but this has proved to be very hard to achieve in any way that lasts for a long period of time. Moses couldn't do it, King David couldn't do it, and now King Josiah was likewise proving himself unable to do it.

"Did you understand what I was talking to Father about last night?" I asked, knowing that some of the descriptions I had used had been deliberately vague.

"It sounded unpleasant," she replied, "but I couldn't see what your father could have to do with it."

Should I tell her all of the unsavoury details? The symbols, the pictures, the predatory behaviour of that woman? If I didn't, she would never understand why it was so important to me. But I knew my mother, and I was certain that she would be unhappy with my father's behaviour if she knew all the details.

So I tried to give more details without giving away too much, but it just didn't work. My descriptions made the room seem more like a small rug-making enterprise than a centre of idolatry and perversion. That woman came across as being more of a pushy shop assistant than a voracious monster.

In the end, I had to give up. I was not willing to tell my mother all of the details, knowing what her response would be. As God's prophet, I unfortunately had to know these things. They would separate me from my family – I was already finding that out – but should I use them to separate a woman from her husband? And so I left her in the comfortable darkness of ignorance and spoke instead of the idol I had destroyed, and the resulting threats of violence. As I described the actions of the "welcoming committee" just outside Anathoth, my mother interrupted.

"When your father said you attacked Benaiah, I thought he meant verbally!" she exclaimed.

"No. Of course, he should have said 'approached in gentle self-defence'," I said glumly. "I took away Benaiah's weapon when he threatened me with it, that's all. He was drunk – it wasn't hard."

The reactions of Benaiah and Chelub also upset my mother, while the threat of a legal charge with resulting punishment fired both her protective instincts and her righteous anger. The idea that someone should be beaten for destroying an idol when the king himself was doing and encouraging the same thing just a short distance away in Jerusalem, seemed quite ridiculous.

In the back of her mind, I suspected that there was also disappointment with her husband for failing to provide any support for me. As far as she was concerned, I was in the right and deserved support from everyone. This she stated openly. However, she would not mention any connection with her husband, the High Priest of Yahweh, or his responsibilities, particularly in Anathoth, a city of Yahweh's priests.

I remember vividly the events of the next few minutes. As we continued to talk, we heard some muffled shouts outside. Had we not been deep in important conversation, we would have gone to investigate, but we didn't. Instead we continued our talk a short while longer, until a knock on the door of the scroll room claimed our undivided attention. I opened the door and found Eliada, the servant who had looked strangely pleased when my father had so angrily condemned me the previous evening, there. This time, the smirk on his face could not be hidden as he informed me that there were some men to see me at the door.

A cold hand seemed to squeeze my heart and for a time I couldn't breathe. The self-appointed protectors of idols had carried out their threats. They must have come to take me away and beat me! Feeling a little stunned, I walked out towards the door of the house, but my mother got there first. She too had deduced what this call must be about.

"What do you want?" she asked brusquely.

Three men, all members of the city council, stood at the door. Two were Levites and capable scribes, obviously sent to do the dirty work, while at the back lurked Benaiah, the uncle of my friend Benaiah, who was chief of the town council.

"We are here on important business, my lady," said the first of the Levites, showing deference to the High Priest's wife.

"We have a notice of charge for your son Jeremiah," said the other, holding out a rolled sheet of papyrus, but not looking at me as I stood partly behind my mother. My mother made no move to accept the scroll from his hand.

"Witnesses are being called," continued the first, "and the charges will be heard tomorrow morning."

"Your son will need to be present for the hearing – and for any possible punishment which may result," concluded the second, and this time he did look at me, holding out the scroll towards me. Would accepting the scroll give credibility to this unprincipled prosecution? I followed my mother's example and kept my hands close by my sides.

"Will King Josiah be called as a witness?" asked my mother, waving away the scroll imperiously.

The scribes looked a little lost at this question, and it was left to Benaiah, the leader, to respond with a bewildered, "What do you mean?"

"King Josiah is destroying idols in Jerusalem," my mother stated firmly. "If you are charging my son with destroying an idol, why not ask the king for his opinion?"

"But the charges are not only for illegal damage to an item of religious property, madam," responded Benaiah, officiously, "but also for an unprovoked attack on a lawfully appointed official of the council."

"You mean yourself?" asked my mother, rather sarcastically.

"Yes, madam, myself," he acknowledged, a little shamefacedly.

"And how were you armed at the time?" pursued my mother.

"All relevant matters will be dealt with in the lawful assembly," said Benaiah, attempting to claim the moral high ground, but sounding unconvincing.

"So you won't be admitting that you were armed with a heavy stick, which you were attempting to use on Jeremiah even though he was unarmed?" asked my mother in a voice that was perilously close to a sneer. "And you won't be calling on King Josiah to express his opinion of idols? No doubt you have also made plans to silence Jeremiah in the hearing."

That last arrow was fired as from a bow drawn at a venture, yet it struck home most forcibly. Benaiah started and the two scribes looked uncomfortable. Clearly plans *had* been made to silence me so that there would be no defence to these trumped-up charges.

"Well, King Josiah shall hear about this!" said my mother regally, although I'm sure that at the time she had no idea how she was going to achieve this.

"Now look here, lady," said Benaiah, "don't be like that. You won't help anyone by interfering in this business."

"I'm not interfering, just asking you why you aren't following our laws of justice," insisted my mother. "It will be up to King Josiah whether he intervenes or not."

"This matter has nothing to do with King Josiah," whined Benaiah.

"It will have soon," said my mother grimly, moving to close the door.

"Wait, lady, wait," begged Benaiah and he stepped towards the door. He spoke quietly to his henchmen, who looked disappointed and started to walk haltingly away. Once they had rounded the corner of our house, he turned back to us and said, "Well, maybe I was a little hasty. Jeremiah is rather young, and has been away from Judah a lot over the last few years. He just needs to learn to respect the property of others, that's all. This time, we will let him off with a warning."

"A warning that I must obey you instead of Yahweh?" I asked.

Benaiah looked at me and snarled, "Just don't touch our gods, young man, that's what I mean." Looking back at my mother, he smiled a sickly smile and said, "Sorry to have troubled you, madam," and turned to walk away.

As we turned away from the door, I caught Eliada the servant with a look of chagrin on his face.

Enemies in my own family. Enemies amongst my friends. Enemies in my village. Enemies in Jerusalem. Enemies amongst the nobles. And now, enemies amongst the family servants as well. Were there any other groups of people among whom I could start collecting enemies?

Oh, my God, am I doing your work so very badly?

☙

My first legal challenge was over, and God had protected me again – this time through the protective care of my mother. I closed the door of the house and turned around to see my mother beckoning to me from the doorway of the scroll room. Hurrying into the room, I closed the door quickly as I heard her start to sob.

Courageous though she had been in the conflict, with never a sign of weakness, her extreme distress could no longer be denied. Throughout the confrontation her words had been crisp and confident; indeed, her introduction of the name of King Josiah had been masterful. She had walked what was, for a woman, a very fine line, and won the battle – but the pressure had told, and it was some time before she could calm herself. What would her husband say when he heard of her exploits? Once the victory was won, this was the thought uppermost in her mind, and I regretted being the cause of her concern.

My father had refused to support me, his son, through these ungodly attacks. Would he support his wife?

Chapter 9

Lessons in Anathoth

It was to be three days before I could return to Jerusalem again. My delayed visits to Gemariah and his family, and to Azariah and his family – both arranged with my mother's help – occupied my afternoons and early evenings for the next two days.

Gemariah was pleased to see me – we had not met for almost a year – but it was also clear that he was fully occupied with his family and his work. With an obvious mix of pride and concern, he presented his son Hasshub, born a few months after my last visit. My mother had warned me that he would not look as healthy as Azariah's son Zadok, although they were almost identical in age. Gemariah's wife Abigail was very gentle with the child and handled him as if he needed very special care.

For the first time ever, I wondered how marriage might fit in with a career as a prophet to the nations, but, for the time being, I put it out of my mind as an unnecessary worry.

Gemariah wanted to talk about the Book of the Law, but his interest was purely technical. He wanted to know how old the scroll was, and had a few ideas as to how we might be able to tell, but he had no burning desire to read its contents. Over the last four years he had continued his preparation for taking a position of leadership in the religious hierarchy of Judah. His house had been provided by our father, and he had a comfortable life of riches with few responsibilities. He had become a "dabbler" – one who got involved in various areas which were of interest to him at the time, but without any driving determination to become expert in them or to be exclusively committed to them. Having, like me, inherited his father's messy handwriting, he had not been in the running for the job of copying the Book of the Law, but I doubt that he would have been interested in doing so anyway, because of the strict demands placed on those scribes.

During our conversation, he suggested that political matters could still have a significant impact on this work. This started to ring warning bells in my head and reminded me that I needed to keep up to date with progress. Surely the copying of God's word would be a challenging but clear-cut task? And surely Josiah's daily visits showed his interest in the book and in making it available to more people, so that nothing could go wrong? Nevertheless, Gemariah's comments put me on my guard, which I was glad of later.

As for my work as a prophet, Gemariah was interested in a token fashion, but family and establishment loomed large in his life and the possibility of direct input from Yahweh was losing its attraction for him. Instead, the physical temple of Yahweh was the centre of his worship. My childhood friends had already taken different paths from me, and now Gemariah, my brother – who was also my friend – was slowly diverging from my path also.

Many times over the years since God had called me, I had thought of Elijah's certainty that he was the only remaining follower of God. God's denial of this with the assurance that 7,000 in Israel still worshipped God had always been a source of great encouragement to me. But what about now? It had been many years after the time of Elijah that Israel had been sent into captivity. How many worshippers of God had been left in Israel by the time the nation was destroyed? 5,000? 500? 50? 5? There was no way to know, yet God had said to me that Judah was now worse than Israel had been. How many true prophets or even believers in Yahweh were left in Judah?

⳹

My visit to Azariah and his family was just what I had expected in many ways: welcoming on a superficial level, but swiftly sinking to supercilious sneers when the discussion began to move into any area he did not like. And that included almost every subject that I could ever be interested in! He was willing to talk about the temple, but only if I would heap unquestioning praise on its state and operation. The temple of the Lord was an end in itself, an eternal sign of God's approval.

Hephzibah was a beautiful woman and Azariah was clearly proud of her. Seraiah was a cute toddler, but it seemed to me that his mother did not want me spending much time with him. She obviously shared Azariah's opinion that I was not a desirable character. Zadok was a happy, healthy looking baby, and the contrast with his cousin Hasshub was quite obvious.

We shared an evening meal and the servants did all the work. There were more servants on show than we had ever had at home. Hephzibah did nothing to help with any preparation, although, in her defence, she did spend some time with her sons instead. However, the maids seemed to do most of the work of caring for the children too. My mother had always arranged the servants, spent time with us children, and still found time to do some of the housework as well. I hoped I was wrong, but the impression I gained from Azariah and Hephzibah was that they considered themselves to be part of the rather idle rich. Servants were their right. Not only that, but the servants must foresee all eventualities and predict any possible needs without being asked. Any commands that had to be given were a sign of failure on the part of the servant and must be obeyed instantly with the right degree of obsequious penitence. Hephzibah seemed to feel a little offended if she needed to issue any commands – why had not the servants anticipated her wishes? It was not done in an overtly cruel fashion, but seemed completely unreasonable all the same.

An example, for which I felt responsible, was when I asked for a drink shortly after my arrival. Hephzibah called a young servant lad and imperiously told him to fetch a drink. Quite naturally, he asked me what I would like to drink, and swiftly brought me the water I requested, presented in a simple cup. This was not good enough for Hephzibah, who was unhappy with the provision of water – it should have been wine – and completely dissatisfied with the simple wooden cup in which the water was provided. I was a visitor, and the servant should have known to use a metal cup. Her words to the lad were not meant for my ears, but I heard them anyway, spoken quietly in a cold voice: "If you can't do a better job than that, you will lose your job with us too, just like your mother did."

Later enquiries, when I met the lad in the street, revealed that his mother had worked in Azariah's house until she had been sent away. Apparently a stain had been found on Seraiah's clothing, and Hephzibah had been certain that it had appeared while he was under the woman's supervision. I also found that the lad's father was dead, and now his mother had no work. Thus, his mother and two younger brothers depended on his work for food.

Azariah's home was spotless and admirably appointed, but it seemed sterile and full of self-importance. No mention was made of God except when I mentioned the Book of the Law, and then the subject was quickly changed.

The current High Priest allowed the worship of other gods in the name of tolerance and cooperation, but what of the next High Priest? To whom would he turn? Even the limited principles of our father seemed to be a little beyond Azariah. Would he find his niche in concentrating on the shallow and pernickety words of ancient scribes, or would he be a leader in name only, leaving the nation rudderless, without any religious leadership at all?

And, critically, what of the Book of the Law? Would he ever read it? Priests were meant to provide teaching and answers to questions about God's law, starting with the grand principles of equity, justice, love and faithfulness – but how could Azariah do that? Our father did not know Yahweh well enough; Azariah knew him even less.

It was a frightening consideration that bounced around in my head as I watched the beautiful smiles and experienced the cultured hospitality on display that evening. A wide and tempting range of foods was served on expensive plates and in beautiful dishes, but the hospitality seemed artificial; more of a finely tuned performance than a natural outpouring of overwhelming generosity such as was shown by a man like Abraham, the friend of God.

In both Gemariah and Azariah I saw the accumulated changes of the last few years. Each was choosing his own way in life, and it seemed to me that neither had God at the centre of his life. A future leading priest and the next High Priest of Israel. In what direction would the worship of Judah progress under their influence?

Oh, Judah, my country! Your doom was so predictable, yet I always hoped it would be otherwise.

◌

By the end of my visit to Azariah's house, I was quite demoralised. Everything should have been wonderful in Judah, with the encouraging discovery of the Book of the Law acting as reinforcement for the faith of a nation.

If I looked only on the bright side, there was so much to be happy about. A humble king who cared about God and wanted to worship him, and a nation that was turning towards God a little and showing it by giving gifts in the temple. The temple itself was beginning to emerge from decades of neglect, with newly polished metalwork and freshly cleaned masonry announcing the change. The repairs were progressing remarkably well.

So why was I so depressed?

Ostriches are impressive birds: big and strong and amazingly fast. But they do not look after their children or worry about the future. Everything they do is for today. The immediate appearance is imposing, but all of that running around can just get you into trouble faster if you don't run in the right direction. A grand appearance can also obscure less palatable details – many an ostrich will lay its eggs and leave them completely alone with no care.

At the moment, my nation was like the ostrich. A grand appearance that looked promising, but distracted attention from details much less attractive.

A temple swarming with busy workmen repairing and cleaning was balanced by the unpleasant behaviour of those inside.

A humble and pious king was balanced by an ignorant and uncaring priesthood.

The guidance from God found in the Book of the Law was balanced by the widespread ignorance of the books we already had.

Josiah's righteous destruction of pagan altars and idols was counteracted by the bustling work of the populace in moving their idols out of his view into hidden places, just waiting for an opportunity to fight back against such restraint.

Every good aspect that I could think of was more than counter-balanced by a negative feature that sprang all too readily to mind.

Was it time to give up and just join the crowd in rushing headlong to destruction?

No. I couldn't do it. King Josiah wasn't giving up, so I shouldn't either. What my nation needed was people who were working tirelessly for God, and equally tirelessly interceding with God for the nation as well. Our traditions told us of Moses' prayer of intercession when Israel had worshipped a golden calf – a prayer that had softened the face of Yahweh. After this, the people had been reclaimed to the worship of God. We really did need another prophet like Moses.

But dwelling on the negatives would not fix them. Encouraging the positives and concentrating on prayer might be able – just possibly – to cure the nation of its backsliding.

My father had returned to Anathoth that evening, and when I returned from Azariah's house, he was able to give me more information about the copying of the Book of the Law. It didn't help my mood, either.

What bothered me most was the news that the committee reviewing the updates that were being made to the Book of the Law were apparently making their decisions on purely technical, linguistic and social grounds. There did not appear to be any reference to existing reliable knowledge about God or his rules. The minor unease I had felt when Gemariah had mentioned possible problems with the work started to grow. We should not – we must not – end up with the book of God's law being corrupted by a collection of expert scribes who would rewrite it to suit their whims[31] and the general usage of society!

This took me away from my thoughts of intercession – it would have to wait until my time of meditation next morning. In the meantime, I must begin to equip myself with a better knowledge of the word of God which was available. There were many, many scrolls that were reputed to be the word of God, but my experience with some of these scrolls during my education made me doubt the veracity of many. The work of cataloguing these works must be done based on their credibility, and I seemed to be better equipped than most to do such a job – despite my youth. Maybe I was just more critical than most.

Our house would be the best place to start. Under the encouraging influence of Josiah, scrolls of God's word had become much easier to find over the last few years. Our scroll room now held many more scrolls than it had done on the day when I first met my scroll of Isaiah and was guided by it into a better understanding of Yahweh. In those days, we would never have had more than ten scrolls in the house, but now we had more than fifty – if the quick count I had made of the stack of scrolls on the table was anything to go by. Many were scrolls from which a new copy had recently been made with the old, worn scrolls ending up in our scroll room because no-one was

---

[31] See Jeremiah 8:8.

really sure what should be done with them. They were all old and some were quite decrepit, but no-one was quite willing to destroy them.

My father's eyesight had been deteriorating in recent years, and he now found reading by lamplight difficult, if not impossible. Thus the scrolls had mounted up, forming the perfect place for me to start. These were old scrolls and each had a history associated with it, if only that history could be unearthed.

If the scrolls had been able to speak, they could have told many different stories. The oldest scrolls would tell of successive kings whose declining interest in the word of Yahweh had been reflected in the life of the nation. They could tell of a gradual transformation whereby they spent more and more of their time on shelves instead of living in the hearts of God's nation.

And as a direct result of this degradation in the spiritual life of Judah, some scrolls could also have told stories of bravery and courage as faithful men and women had found it necessary to protect these scrolls from the ravages of Manasseh and earlier evil kings.

The damage of evil scribes must not be ignored either. When scrolls are copied, there is great power in the pen of the scribe. Honest scribes produce honest copies. Perjured scribes work for their masters, whoever they are, and their copies are subtly or openly twisted. Finding and destroying these dishonest copies was the work I was contemplating. However, before I made any commitment to the work, I wanted to review a large number of scrolls to get a sense of the scale of the task.

If we do not feed on God's word when it is easily available, the time will come – it always does – when it can only be found through bravery and courage. King Josiah's reign was a time when reading Yahweh's word was easy, but I knew that it wouldn't last forever. And how much had the word already been obscured by malicious scribes, or by committees like the one now reviewing the Book of the Law?

Ostriches do not care for their young because they know no better. The priests, prophets and kings of Judah all knew much of what God expected. Were they like ostriches, or were they more like wolves, feeding on defenceless innocents?

My feeling of depression and disappointment left me as I began to feel that there was something useful I could do. I mentioned to my father my wish to read and categorise the scrolls in the scroll room and, for once, he seemed quite pleased by a suggestion I had made. Maybe he felt that this would keep me out of trouble and focus my thoughts on history rather than on prophesying about the future. Whatever the reason, I was able to go into the scroll room with my father's permission to read and study any of the scrolls I found there. Not only that, but he added, "And don't forget the scrolls in the box under the table – there are many more there too. A group of scribes who are priests reviewed a large collection of scrolls, and the scrolls in the box are ones that they did not consider to be very reliable. That is why they are being kept separate."

I picked up a lamp and we went into the scroll room together. Once I had lit the lamp above the desk, my father pointed out all of the places in the room where religious scrolls were kept: a pile of scrolls on the desk, the box under the desk which he had described, and another two boxes in a cupboard beside the desk. I had thought that I would have about fifty scrolls to review, but now I found that there might be hundreds of these valuable treasures.

"And, Jeremiah," my father continued, "you may like to look at the scrolls in this smaller box too. They were brought down from Jerusalem just a few days before you came home. I haven't had a chance to look at them yet, but I believe they were brought back from Israel when King Josiah visited there in his thirteenth year[32]. Some of the scrolls contain the words of various prophets, I think, and others are bits of history. If you could look at them for me, it would be a great help. We need to know what they are and what can be learned from them – if anything."

My excitement had risen higher with every item that he showed me. Fifty scrolls had seemed a marvellous starting point, but now I had what seemed to be a massive treasure-trove of new and old scrolls, including the word of God to prophets in the north. It was already getting quite late by this time, but I couldn't wait to study these scrolls.

Removing the lid of the smaller box, I lifted the first scroll from the top. It was a small papyrus scroll, without any wrappings around it, and tied with a simple cord. Undoing the cord, I gently unrolled the scroll. It was a list of names or descriptions, each followed by a scroll identifier such as a scribe would use, and after reading through it a few times, I guessed that it was a manifest of the scrolls in the box. The descriptions included names like Hosea, Amos and Nahum, as well as titles like "The Chronicles of the Kings of Israel". Some of the names I recognised as prophets whose writings I knew, but others I did not know, and I had no idea what some of the descriptions might mean.

"I'll leave you now, Jeremiah," said my father, after a while, "but don't stay up too late. I am hoping that you

---

[32] There is no evidence in the Bible for any collection of scrolls being brought to Judah from Israel at any time.

will be able to come with me to Jerusalem again tomorrow."

It was rude of me, but I was completely distracted and did not respond at all as he walked out of the room. In fact, I didn't even notice that he had gone until quite some time later. I had expected to spend only a short time in scanning a few of these scrolls, but the attraction was too great. How could I resist unrolling each of them and reading as much as possible? All were old, there was no doubt about that, and I imagined that they must all have been written before the destruction of the nation of Israel, which had happened almost a century before.

I read and read and read, recognising some of the words as old friends and greeting the rest as new friends, messengers of knowledge and understanding. I worked my way through scroll after scroll, matching the identification of each scroll with the name of its author, so that I knew what I was reading. Time passed, but I could not put the scrolls down. My evening prayers never happened, although the time was spent in the warmth of the presence of God as his words came to me through the scrolls. After a few hours, the light of the lamp began to flicker and grow dim, and I realised that it was running out of oil. Fortunately, there was another lamp on the desk; quickly lighting it, I snuffed out the other and kept reading.

Fascination and excitement filled the night hours. I had never heard much of the history of Israel which I was now reading, and some of the prophecies were also completely new to me. Although I had read much, there was still much left to be read when I noticed a dim light coming through the shutters. Night was over. Morning had come, and normally I would be just getting out of bed. I almost decided to keep on reading, but then I remembered my plan for prayer this morning: intercession. My nation was floundering in idolatry and had no idea where to find Yahweh – or even why they should look for him. God had predicted destruction, but would he be willing to forgive if those of us who loved his law would pray for the nation? My friends had turned to idolatry, my brothers were not equipped to guide the nation as priests, the townsfolk in Anathoth were leaning towards idolatry, and God's judgement would come quickly if nothing changed soon.

I blew out the lamp and silently made my way out of the scroll room before heading outside into the grey dawn. As I walked along the path, it occurred to me to wonder whether the attitude in Anathoth was a reflection of the difference between the simple folk who lived in small towns and the more sophisticated people who lived in the country's capital, Jerusalem. Had Josiah achieved better success with the sort of people who lived in Jerusalem? I certainly hoped so.

Chapter 10

Words from God

Already the sky was growing pink in the west, coloured by the sun as it rose in the east. Autumn clouds wore a halo of dim light around their fringes, while at their heart the darkness of night still lingered.

This morning there was no Benaiah to upset my plans for prayer, so I walked to the pile of stones and sat down on the comfortably smooth stone on top. Overhead, flocks of birds were travelling south as they always did at this time of year, and their calls from far above made a lonely chorus in the spreading dawn. Birds follow the wisdom of instinct which God puts into them. If only we as people would use the wisdom God has put in us by acknowledging a creator – and then searching him out to know him! As I looked out towards the sunrise and the mountains of Moab, I knew that the creation spread out before me could never have been made by the array of gods worshipped across the world. That contrary assortment of conflicting deities could never have agreed on anything, yet the creation showed the hand of a master craftsman, with authority to work as he chose.

I wondered, not for the first time, whether the birds flying above me had made an early start for the day or had been flying throughout the night. There was so much about creation that I did not understand: I could not even understand the people amongst whom I lived. It seemed to me that Judah would be a better place if all of its people worshipped the true God. Yahweh is a forgiving God, but he is also a God of judgement, as my readings throughout the night had reminded me. Would he forgive Judah?

By this time I had made myself comfortable and was ready to pray for my nation, but suddenly there was a change within and around me. I have tried to describe before how it feels when God speaks to me: the burning fire inside that seems to cleanse me from within – to terrify, but cheer. But there are also nuances in the emotion that accompanies the presence of God. At times he has made it very clear that he is not pleased with me; when I have been fighting his directions, arguing with his judgements, or justifying my behaviour. Those times can feel a little like past interviews with my father, when, as a child, I knew that I had done something wrong. But there have also been times when God's presence has wrapped me tightly in his love and rewarded me for courageous obedience.

At some times, however, his presence has pulsated with an anger that is frightening in its intensity, even when it has not been directed at me. That was how the fire of God pulsed in me at this time. The beauty of his ordered creation was swept aside, replaced by a vision of darkness as he spoke to me about the one part of his creation that seemed to choose never to obey – mankind.

> "Stand in the gate of the Lord's house,
> and proclaim there this word, and say,

Hear the word of the Lord, all you men of Judah
who enter these gates to worship the Lord.
Thus says the Lord of hosts, the God of Israel:
Amend your ways and your deeds,
and I will let you dwell in this place."[33]

Despite the anger in God's voice, my first response was a surge of hope! Surely King Josiah would lead us to God as a nation and God would let Judah stay in the land? The temple could genuinely be a place of glorious worship, just as my family liked to proclaim. But in my optimism, I had gone far ahead of God's words. The fire suddenly grew terrifyingly intense and his words burned to my very core. I could think of nothing but his voice as he continued to give me the words I was to speak.

"Do not trust in these deceptive words:
'This is the temple of the Lord,
the temple of the Lord,
the temple of the Lord.'
For if you truly amend your ways and your deeds,
if you truly execute justice one with another,
if you do not oppress the sojourner,
the fatherless, or the widow,
or shed innocent blood in this place,
and if you do not go after other gods to your own harm,
then I will let you dwell in this place,
in the land that I gave of old to your fathers forever."[34]

Later reflection convinced me that God's attitude toward the temple was not one of unquestioning approval. In fact, the future of the temple would be decided by the strength of our desire for justice and by our treatment of each other. If we worshipped other gods,

---

[33] Jeremiah 7:2-3
[34] Jeremiah 7:4-7

our creator would not let us continue to live in the land he had promised to Abraham.

God's words continued, although the anger I feared had abated a little.

"Behold, you trust in deceptive words to no avail.
Will you steal, murder, commit adultery,
swear falsely, make offerings to Baal,
and go after other gods that you have not known,
and then come and stand before me in this house,
which is called by my name, and say, 'We are delivered!'
— only to go on doing all these abominations?
Has this house, which is called by my name,
become a den of robbers in your eyes?
Behold, I myself have seen it, declares the Lord."[35]

The voice paused, as if God was giving me time to think about the words I would be speaking for him. God had said "deceptive words", which must refer to the thrice-repeated line "the temple of the Lord." In what way were those words deceptive? It could be their suggestion of permanence for the building, or it could be the implied connection between the temple and Yahweh. Maybe the words were deceptive because God could choose to depart from the temple and cut all ties with it, so that it was no longer the temple of Yahweh, but an empty, useless shell. Three hundred years had passed since Solomon had built the temple, and its massive stones had always been a symbol of the ongoing, immovable love of God for Israel. Could God really abandon his temple and remove his name from Jerusalem?

God's temple was still used for the worship of God, and King Josiah actively encouraged this. Sacrifices were made every day and worshippers brought gifts to express their thanks to God, but the temple was not buzzing with

---

[35] Jeremiah 7:8-11

joyous adoration as it had been when Solomon built it. History tells us of vast crowds at the dedication of the temple, the fire of God consuming the offerings and the glory of God filling the temple.[36]

But in my lifetime, the temple had always been a quiet place, and even now, most of the increased bustle in the temple revolved around the workmen carrying out repairs – repairs made necessary by generations of neglect. God's temple was certainly not the centre of Judah's life, nor was God himself the god to whom the eyes of the nation turned as their sovereign. Instead, God was worshipped "just in case": love and devotion were given to the more popular, less restrictive gods like Baal, and many people came to God's temple just to make sure that they had covered all possible options. "We are delivered" they would say, and go back to their homes to continue their lives of unrestrained disobedience to Yahweh's laws of love and faithfulness. They would not return to his temple again until another crisis demanded a more extensive consultation of the full spread of all available gods. Yahweh had not been completely abandoned, but he had become a god of last resort.

Yet, through all of this, God had continued to care for his people – from a distance. No glory filling the temple as it had at the start, but still a caring presence such as only Yahweh can provide. Not for God the short-tempered and angry responses of humans, where fists or weapons are so swiftly used when people upset us. Was it patience? God's laws remain, the temple remains, popular indifference remains, and the nation continues as it chooses, without God taking much obvious action at all. Was this patience, or simply an acceptance that humans will do what they do – and it normally won't be good?

---

[36] 2 Chronicles 7:1

The presence of God – the consuming fire within me – waited as I fumbled my way through this mix of thoughts. Now his words continued, still seeming angry with my nation, but also somewhat resigned, as if describing an inevitable future:

> "Go now to my place that was in Shiloh,
> where I made my name dwell at first,
> and see what I did to it
> because of the evil of my people Israel.
> And now, because you have done all these things,
> declares the Lord,
> and when I spoke to you persistently you did not listen,
> and when I called you, you did not answer,
> therefore I will do to the house that is called by my
> name,
> and in which you trust,
> and to the place that I gave to you and to your fathers,
> as I did to Shiloh.
> And I will cast you out of my sight,
> as I cast out all your kinsmen,
> all the offspring of Ephraim."[37]

Another pause, as God's words reached this unwelcome conclusion. Somehow, I knew that this was the end of the message I was to deliver to the people. The sentence of destruction had been pronounced. God had begun with, "Amend your ways and I will let you live in this place," but he had finished by saying that the temple in Jerusalem would be destroyed and the nation driven away. God's patience was at an end and the final judgement had been announced. But could God be persuaded to extend his patience? Would he give more time, or maybe even forgive, if people now prayed as Moses had? I was just working up my courage to begin

---

[37] Jeremiah 7:12-15

speaking to God, when he spoke again and took away all of my hopes:

> "As for you, do not pray for this people,
>   or lift up a cry or prayer for them,
> and do not intercede with me, for I will not hear you."[38]

No prayer for my people? This command was a complete shock to me. The opportunity to pray for others had always been available to all, and many had taken advantage of it. Abraham[39], Moses[40], Job[41] and Samuel[42] had all interceded for others. Some had even been commanded to do so, and Samuel had said that it would be a sin for him *not* to do so, but now *I must not pray for my people.* Yet I was to be a priest! Surely a priest is to stand between God and man, arguing with the people on God's behalf, while also begging God to be patient with the people. Why must I not? The flames were almost gentle as Yahweh continued:

> "Do you not see what they are doing
> in the cities of Judah and in the streets of Jerusalem?"[43]

And as he spoke, visions of the behaviour he described passed before my eyes:

> "The children gather wood, the fathers kindle fire,
>   and the women knead dough,
> to make cakes for the queen of heaven.
> And they pour out drink offerings to other gods,
>   to provoke me to anger.
> Is it I whom they provoke? declares the Lord.
> Is it not themselves, to their own shame?
> Therefore thus says the Lord God:

---

[38] Jeremiah 7:16
[39] Genesis 18:22-32; 20:7
[40] Exodus 32:9-14
[41] Job 1:5; 42:7-10
[42] 1 Samuel 12:19-23
[43] Jeremiah 7:17

> behold, my anger and my wrath will be poured out
> on this place, upon man and beast,
> upon the trees of the field and the fruit of the ground;
> it will burn and not be quenched."[44]

God's answer to my unspoken thoughts had pointed to the behaviour, not of the leaders, but of the ordinary people of Judah. This was no evil led by the king, his nobles, the priests or false prophets; it was the action and feelings of the nation as a whole. The brightness of his presence spoke of the destruction which would come in his overflowing anger. The fire I felt within me would be reflected in an unquenchable fire that would burn to desolation, and I saw fleeting pictures of this also: brief, disjointed instants of consuming confusion, of armies and death. Judah was doomed, and I could not even pray for mercy. All that there was to be thankful for was the delay which King Josiah had brought about through his humility.

How long would King Josiah live? He was still a young man – only twenty-six years old. Already he had reigned for eighteen years, but he could easily continue to reign for another forty years. These were the optimistic thoughts that filled my mind that autumn morning. Only time would tell, and sadly, the tale it has told has been much less optimistic. In fact, at that time, only thirty-five years remained for the kingdom of Judah, before God's anger and wrath were poured out; burning, burning, until the nation was reduced to ashes.

The words and the anger of God continued within me. I could no longer argue, no longer question – even the patience of God has an end, and, as a nation, we had used up all that was available in the vast well of God's patience.

---

[44] Jeremiah 7:18-20

God spoke to me of sacrifices and reminded me that sacrifices were never the aim of his commands. God did not want sacrifices from his nation, since they were only needed when obedience had already failed. Instead, what God wanted was obedience[45].

As a nation at that time, if our worship of God concentrated on anything, it was on sacrifices and offerings. Yet God was saying that we could keep them all – he didn't want them. All he wanted was obedience. Simple, honest obedience. We had offered sacrifices instead.

> "From the day that your fathers
> came out of the land of Egypt to this day,
> I have persistently sent all my servants the prophets
> to them, day after day."[46]

Over the years, God had sent vast numbers of prophets. Many are not even named in the historical records, but God sent them persistently. In fact, his expression "day after day" had the sense of getting up early to do something urgent. Every day since the time of Moses, God had been urgently sending messengers to warn his people. Some had been killed and others imprisoned, while a very few had had small moments of success; overall, though, God's message had been ignored and his servants mistreated. And, of course, this was happening to me as well. However, I had the singular blessing of a promise that if I stood up to them, they would never overcome me.

Never before had God allowed me so much thinking time in the middle of his instructions. But finally, he continued:

---

[45] Jeremiah 7:21-24
[46] Jeremiah 7:25

"So you shall speak all these words to them,
but they will not listen to you.
You shall call to them,
but they will not answer you."[47]

Yes, the hopelessness of my mission was made very clear to me quite early in my career as a prophet. I knew my work was doomed to fail. God did not hide it from me, but nor did he allow me to give up when I found that I could not win the battle. He had shaped me and my life from the very beginning so that I could be a prophet to the nations, and a prophet I must be – even when failure was guaranteed. Maybe individuals would listen. Or maybe it was more about learning some of the patient waiting of God who warns and waits for centuries. For me, patience used to be about not losing my temper for a few minutes. God has taught me at least to measure patience in decades, while he continues to measure it in centuries or millennia. Patience is hard to live.

---

[47] Jeremiah 7:27

Chapter 11

Old words and new

My father's plans for that day were simple: he wanted to get me back onto the path of preparing to be a priest. He also felt confident that he had a good scheme to coax me to cooperate.

As we walked to Jerusalem, we passed the former home of the idol I had destroyed. Work was already underway to build a more substantial shrine than the makeshift one I had destroyed. It was hard to control a thrill of fear as I wondered what sort of confrontation might arise over this in the future.

The weather was fine and sunny, and countless birds flew in large flocks across the cloudless sky. An autumn sun does not have the brutal power of mid-summer when walking in the hills of Judah can be akin to walking in an oven, but even so, the early morning sun was quite hot. We passed between Har Hatsophim and the Mount of Olives and again looked down on Jerusalem. Although it was only three days since my last visit, the accumulating changes to the temple seemed to stand out. Even more gleaming metalwork reflected the morning sun, and the stonework looked several shades lighter in many places where stones must have been replaced.

Again, my father was eager to point out the beauties of the temple and to highlight the work that was being done. As High Priest, he was very pleased with the attention "his" temple was receiving. While we walked down towards the city gate, he began to explain exactly what he wanted me to do that day, and so I heard for the first time of the honey with which he was baiting his little trap. It was cunning alright, and he was very sure that I would not be able to refuse his request. He was right.

We were going to the scroll room in the temple, where my father wanted me to join the group of scribes reviewing the copied sheets of parchment of the Book of the Law. One of the appointed Validators came from the south of Judah and had received news that his aged father had fallen seriously ill and was unlikely to recover. He had immediately returned to his home and it was not known when he would return. As a result, there was a vacancy amongst the Validators. My father had used his influence to give me the right of first refusal for the position. He was confident that this would be a good way to get me involved in the work of the temple, and he probably hoped that it would lead me to join my brothers in a priestly career. I have no doubt that he also hoped I would calm down and stop my radical prophesying and trouble-making. Once I had started to calm down, no doubt he would be able to appoint me to a good job in the temple, marry me to a nice Levite girl and whisper a quiet prayer of thanks that the prodigal son had grown up. As things turned out, it didn't take long for his plan to go awry, but neither of us knew that at the time.

Looking at the appointment impartially, I was not very well qualified for the work of review. Nevertheless, I was confident that my commitment to God's word, and the knowledge I had of it through consistent reading over the past four years, would overcome my lack of expertise. My only real doubt that day was whether I would be able to stay awake, after my all-night vigil reading the scrolls from Israel!

Once my father had explained his plan, my step quickened and I had to consciously slow down so that I would not leave him behind. I was eager to get to the scroll room, and very eager to start reading the Book of the Law.

☙

Passing through the Benjamin Gate and the matching gate of the temple, we found our way to the scroll room, where work for the day had already started.

The validation of the first set of copied sheets had been mostly completed over the last two days while I had stayed in Anathoth. Two sheets still needed checking by one last Validator, and this was to be my task for the day. My father led me to the corner of the room where the Validators were sitting. They had each completed their part of checking the first copy, and so they were now working on other tasks, but such was the importance of this project that they were all still present – just in case they were needed. I sat at an empty table and my father gave me a scroll.

"You'll need this," he said. "In the meantime, Immer and I need to join the rest of the review committee to discuss the questions and comments that the Validators have raised over the last few days."

Since the sheets to be verified were the first copies that had been made and the text had been updated in the process, the new copy had to be checked against the original copy read in conjunction with a list of abbreviations and word changes that had been prepared by the review committee. This was the scroll my father had given me. It included the changes that were considered necessary to bring the Book of the Law up to date with our modern usage of script and language. The preparation of this list and its subsequent application to the Book of the Law had been causing considerable delays and disputation.

To be successful in comparing the copied sheet with the original and the list of approved changes, I needed to be familiar with the list first. This was quite a lengthy document containing many lines of the form:

"*Replace 'x' with 'y'* ".

Some cases were more detailed:

"*Replace 'x' with 'y' except when…*".

And I was utterly amazed to see that some lines towards the end were open-ended instructions like:

"*Replace words of total condemnation with expressions which match modern inclusive usage*" and "*Replace extremist rhetoric with more moderate wording.*"

What did this mean in practice, and how could it ever succeed anyway? Was it to be left up to each scribe to decide what "*modern inclusive usage*" was, or would the committee meet to review every sheet and possibly demand new copies if they did not like the form of "*modern inclusive usage*" chosen by the scribe? No wonder there had been hints of conflicts and disagreements! One of the Validators was sitting by the wall near me, a very widely experienced older Levite named Meshullam who had occasionally taught us organisational and supervisory skills. He was watching my face as I came to the end of the list, and my expression must have revealed my feelings.

"Just a little vague, isn't it, young Jeremiah?" he asked with a smile.

"It's impossible," I responded frankly, shaking my head in disbelief. "How can anyone follow these instructions and get it right first time? And what is 'right' anyway?"

"The review committee is the final arbiter of what is 'right'. And they have been making sure that the scribes and Validators know their opinions so that no nasty surprises come up," he replied, with a wry smile. He had been a good teacher and was currently helping to supervise the repair work being undertaken in the temple. His involvement in the work of validation reflected his wide range of abilities and his particular interest in the Book of the Law.

"Well, I haven't heard their opinions," I replied, "and my first reading of this list isn't inspiring me with confidence."

"You must do what your conscience dictates, Jeremiah," said Meshullam, surprisingly. "But don't cause any more trouble than you have to."

His words sounded like wise advice, and I kept them in mind as I read through the list one more time and then started to compare the original scroll with the updated copy. To do a proper job of validating, I thought it would be best to read in small sections, first reading from the original sheet and then reading the new copy. In that way, I would quickly see just how difficult it was to read the ancient script, and also begin to see how much difference the modernisations made.

Surprisingly, I found the old script a joy to read: both as an intellectual challenge and as a nostalgic connection with a past in which Yahweh's words had been valued more highly. Quaint and artistic abbreviations were found among occasional detailed expansions of various modern words which I had not even realised were abbreviations. Reading the original for the first time was a pleasure which had little to do with its content. Reading the updated copy, however, made me notice the content. It was the fifth sheet of the Book of the Law and began with warnings against forgetting Yahweh and failing to keep his commandments[48]. Before long, I felt that I was noticing a trend. Words which you might describe as absolute were being watered down. Clear words of command were becoming a little less demanding. Words of condemnation were being softened, somehow, and any demands for exclusive worship of God seemed to be particularly popular targets.

I glanced across at Meshullam again and found that he was watching me. "I have already reviewed that sheet, Jeremiah," he said quietly.

"Did you make any comments?" I asked.

"Yes, quite a few," he answered, "but I was overruled."

"When I first heard of this whole copying job, it sounded easy," I mused.

"Yes," he agreed, "I felt the same."

"Maybe an exact copy would be better, despite all the archaisms and obscure language," I said thoughtfully.

"But then the ordinary people will not understand it and will need people to explain it. And those 'people'," he waved his hand around the room inclusively, "will explain it in the way you read it there… and in all of the other sheets," he finished, drily.

"Some of the changes are so small that they can be easily corrected," I said. "For example, when God warns of destruction if we worship other gods, he says 'And if you forget the Lord your God and go after other gods and

---

[48] Deuteronomy 8:11-20

serve them and worship them'[49], the last part of which has been changed to '…go after other gods and serve *only* them and worship *only* them'. The word '*only*' has been added twice and must simply be removed again. That is easy – and utterly essential! God doesn't condemn idol worship only when it excludes him. He always condemns it."

"I noticed that change myself," responded Meshullam, "but I didn't object because that is the way such ideas are often expressed in our scrolls."

"Not in the originals, it isn't," I insisted. "Yahweh demands exclusive worship from us." Suddenly it struck me that in the bustle of the morning I had somehow forgotten God's command for me to speak at the gates of the temple. How could I have forgotten it? I had never forgotten any such instruction from God before. Were God's words becoming so common to me that I was not treating them with the awe and respect they deserved? I didn't think so, but I couldn't find any other way to account for having forgotten such a clear and simple instruction. "Yahweh commanded me to speak on that very subject just this morning," I continued, distractedly, "and I must go and speak at the gates of the temple as soon as I have finished reviewing this sheet."

"Jeremiah," said Meshullam urgently, "I need to see some other scrolls that support this idea. If you can show me some, I will happily join you in fighting this battle."

"But Meshullam," I argued, "how many times do we read this idea in the Book of the Law itself? You have read it all: is this the only place?"

Meshullam leaned back against the wall and looked thoughtful. "No, I suppose it is not the only example," he mused. "I can think of at least three other places

---

[49] Deuteronomy 8:19

containing the same idea. In fact, one of them is much more detailed and explicit than this section." He stood up and walked across to the small stack of sheets of parchment that sat on a table nearby. These were the updated copies that had already been checked by ten Validators. He selected one and came back.

"This is the sheet," he said, placing it on the table in front of me and pointing to a section of text. "This is what it says, and notice the word '*only*': '…all the host of heaven, you be drawn away and bow down *only* to them and serve *only* them'[50]. In the original, the word '*only*' does not occur. Minimal change for maximum effect."

"The word 'only' should not be there at all," I stated, definitely; "and it must go!" I concluded, categorically.

Meshullam looked at me and pursed his lips grimly, before relaxing, smiling gently, and saying, "I don't like our chances of winning this argument – or any argument like it, to be honest. But I think we have to try."

"Meshullam, you said that that passage was even more explicit than the one I started with. Were those two words the only changes made?"

"Yes," he replied, "the other parts are just explained away as having a different meaning from the obvious one. The words are:

" 'Therefore watch yourselves very carefully. Since you saw no form on the day that the Lord spoke to you at Horeb out of the midst of the fire, beware lest you act corruptly by making a carved image for yourselves, in the form of any figure, the likeness of male or female, the likeness of any animal that is on the earth, the likeness of any winged bird that flies in the air, the likeness of

---

[50] Deuteronomy 4:19

anything that creeps on the ground, the likeness of any fish that is in the water under the earth.'[51]

"These words seem to completely forbid the making of any likeness of anything to worship it, but the committee argues that it should be read to refer to making images to help worship Yahweh," Meshullam continued. "They say that Yahweh does not want us to make any images of *him*, but that images for other gods are acceptable as long as we continue to worship Yahweh as well. That is the importance of those two extra *'only*'s. If you take them out, the meaning is very clear – and quite different from what the committee wants it to mean."

"Yes," I said slowly. "And this is done through the entire book?"

"It is," responded Meshullam, definitely, "along with many other changes that we should talk about once you have reviewed this sheet." He paused and tugged at his beard, "And I was willing to accept those changes," he finished with disgust.

"It makes me very suspicious of any changes that have been made," I mused, "but some of the changes should be a great help in understanding the Book of the Law. I suppose that I need to go through this sheet letter by letter and do the job I am meant to be doing."

Meshullam agreed and went back to his work with another scroll, while I resumed my checking.

☙

Later in the morning I was torn between two utterly essential tasks: delivering the words of God at the gate of the temple, and fighting against the corruption of the Book of the Law of Yahweh. The former had been kept

---

[51] Deuteronomy 4:15-18

waiting by my inexplicable memory lapse, but must wait no longer. The latter? – Every letter of every word on the sheet had been checked and, as expected, I had found no copying errors. However, I had made a list of "updates" that I had questions about. Many would be acceptable as single changes on their own, but taken together, they seemed to change the tenor of the text and skew its meaning in a particular direction. But these questions would have to wait.

Whenever God had spoken to me in the past, there had always been a strong urge to do something about it, and it made me wonder what had been so different this morning. My only possible answer was that God must have wanted me to check the words of the Book of the Law first. Whatever the reason, the desire to do something about the words that God had spoken was now very strong within me. Irresistible, in fact.

Since neither Immer nor my father was yet available, I left a message with one of the other Validators that I would be at the gate of the temple, delivering a message from Yahweh to the worshippers. Meshullam left with me as he wanted to check briefly on the progress of some repair work which had been delayed by late deliveries of materials.

Leaving the room, we parted immediately; Meshullam walked towards the Benjamin Gate of the temple through which my father had led me that morning, while I found my way to one of the gates on the other side of the temple. The door of the room where the women did their weaving was closed, but I walked past it as quickly as possible. What should be done about this room was still an open question in my mind, and I prayed a quick prayer for guidance as I hurried past. At that moment, however, the words God had spoken were welling up in me and I was sure that he wanted obedience from me first – now was the time to deliver his message to the worshippers who passed through this, the most popular gate of the temple.

The sun was directly overhead as I climbed onto a low wall near the gate of the temple and began to claim the attention of the worshippers passing through. The sun shone brilliantly on piles of building materials inside the gates. New deliveries were being made all the time.

In the wilderness, God had ordered the completion of all of the components of the tabernacle before it was assembled and sanctified as a centre of worship. Repairs were not even mentioned. Did this mean that repairs would never be necessary in a hallowed place of worship? Or was it just that the tabernacle was to be assembled and disassembled often enough that repairs could be made while it was not in use?

Whatever had happened in the wilderness, worshippers now mingled with busy workers as they came to pray, make sacrifices and present more gifts for the ongoing refurbishment of the temple.

The temple was undoubtedly a busier place than when I had stood in this same gateway more than four years before. At that time in the spring of the thirteenth year of King Josiah, chill winds had made my job quite uncomfortable, but now the chill winds had gone and the audience would be much larger. There was also a happier feeling on the streets and people were more ready to smile than had been the case when Josiah's reforms had started. Sunny weather probably helped too!

> " 'Hear the word of the Lord, all you men of Judah who enter these gates to worship the Lord.'[52]"

Once I started speaking, the familiar fire burned and the glowing words were clear in my mind to guide me

---

[52] Jeremiah 7:2

through every phrase. But this time, the anger of God's message began to build up inside me too.

At the same time, I also found myself seeking to understand the feelings of a worshipper who had come to make a sacrifice to God or give a gift for the temple. Maybe such visitors were responding to their king's encouragement to worship Yahweh. How would they understand the message Yahweh was giving to his people? I imagined that they might feel insulted, hard-done-by and unjustly treated. After all, they had chosen to come to God's temple, when so many others never came at all. It wasn't hard to imagine them thinking to themselves, "How dare this prophet stand there and tell me off!"

For a time, I didn't really feel completely in control of my thoughts. It was as if God was trying to show me the contrast between his feelings and those of the worshippers, helping me to see the vast gulf between these two conflicting outlooks.

What a terribly intense clash of opinions fought within my mind that afternoon! I felt that each point of view could make sense, but could I bring the two together? I am ashamed to say that for a time I felt more sympathy for the feelings of the worshippers as I imagined them than for the demanding words of God. Above all, though, I felt sorry for myself, having to be the man in the middle between two immovable opponents.

Somehow, throughout this conflict – which takes much longer to describe than it took to experience – I also continued to repeat the words God had given me. I came to the words:

> " 'Will you steal, murder, commit adultery,
>   swear falsely, make offerings to Baal,
> and go after other gods that you have not known,
> and then come and stand before me in this house,

which is called by my name, and say, "We are delivered!" — only to go on doing all these abominations?'[53]"

And as I spoke the words, small pictures flitted through my mind of all the evil behaviour that I was describing. I saw a picture of money being callously stolen and then a part of it being carried through the gates of the temple to give to God. A man heard my words as he passed and looked at me blandly without response, yet I could see in his pocket a small bag holding the stolen money.

In another scene, two sheep were selected from the flock: one was offered to Baal and the other brought through the gate of the temple of Yahweh. At that instant, I saw a man leading a lamb through the gate of the temple and knew that God was opening my eyes to see the truth of the words he wanted me to speak.

Pictures continued along with the words, and I saw a man in the gateway who had murdered his brother to get his inheritance, and knew also that he had not come to the temple seeking forgiveness.

An older man came in with the stream of people and I saw the scene of lying evidence which had caused his neighbour to be executed for a murder he had not committed. "Yahweh bless you," he called out to another, whom I recognised as his accomplice in the crime, even now approaching the gate of Yahweh's temple.

A scene reminiscent of Solomon's words in Proverbs came to my mind: I saw a young man walking along a street at dusk, saw him greeted by a woman I recognised, with painted face and brazen tongue[54]. As he eagerly followed her inside and shut the door behind him, he passed out of the picture in my mind and entered instead

---

[53] Jeremiah 7:9-10
[54] Proverbs 7:7-27

the view of my waking eyes, as the very same man walked past me into the temple.

God had made his point. Many of those who came to the house of Yahweh came on their own terms. For them, this was not God's holy house, but a house for unrepentant robbers.

Chapter 12

"Updates" updated

Already tired from a sleepless night, by the end of that day, I was utterly exhausted.

But an important victory had been won.

After repeating the words of Yahweh for a second and a third time at the gate of the temple, I had returned to the scroll room to find a serious argument in progress.

My father and Immer had finished their meeting with the other members of the review committee. Apparently the meeting had come to a majority decision to support all of the "updates" that had been made to the Book of the Law, but the length of the meeting suggested that there had been differences of opinion.

Meshullam, meanwhile, had spent some time checking on the temple repair work. The change of focus seemed to have helped him to make up his mind about the so-called "updates" because he had apparently returned to the scroll room determined to force a re-evaluation of the changes. He had spoken to several other Validators and scribes about them and found that some were not completely happy with the alterations that were being made to the text.

Others supported the changes, though, and the subsequent discussions showed that many of these scribes had no commitment to the Book of the Law as the word of Yahweh at all. In fact, the majority viewed the Book of the Law as an interesting historical artefact, but nothing more. This became the basis for a new argument, with Meshullam and a few others arguing that anyone who did not believe that these were the words of Yahweh should withdraw from the process completely, since they could not treat the text with the respect it deserved!

This, of course, was heaping fuel on the fire as the unbelieving scribes spoke of "professionalism", "integrity" and so on. A ding-dong verbal battle had been in full swing when my father entered, and it might have descended to fisticuffs if he had not arrived when he did. The scribes and Validators all showed my father the respect warranted by his position as High Priest, and each of the conflicting groups was eager to explain the situation and establish the strength of their own position. Shortly afterwards, Immer had also returned, and by the time I arrived, Meshullam had won some support. The group of unbelievers had agreed together on one point though: it was all my fault! As I entered the room the antagonism was palpable, and many muttered comments were thrown in my direction.

My father and Immer had each been asked by both sides of the argument whether they believed that the Book of the Law was genuinely the word of God. But both were blessed with tworldly wisdom at least, and had refused to answer the question.

The unbelieving scribes were protesting their ability to do the job well despite their unbelief, while also finding opportunities to sneer at those who did believe. As I listened, I was struck by what seemed to me a conflict: why bother with copying and updating the scroll so carefully if its contents were of purely historical interest anyway? Working hard to copy the words of Yahweh correctly made sense to me, but for those who did not believe it to be the word of God, this job was merely a professional achievement, something to boast to their grandchildren about. A shallow aim indeed!

My father tried to bring the argument back to its original starting place: were the agreed content updates valid? Some argued strongly in their favour, while others denounced them as anti-Yahweh. The opposing groups were largely the same as the sides in the argument about whether the Book of the Law was the word of Yahweh or not, though a few doubting scribes were evidently trying to exercise their "professionalism" and "integrity" by weighing the evidence somewhat more impartially.

As the argument raged back and forth, the amount of support for including the categoric statements found in the Book of the Law gradually increased. Internal consistency within the book itself was taken into account, and increasing numbers of old scrolls which exhibited the same characteristics were referred to.

Voices were still raised in anger from time to time, but overall the discussion was gradually calming down when, unexpectedly, King Josiah and his entourage quietly entered the room.

It was earlier than his daily inspection of the copying work – a re-scheduled meeting had made the normal time impossible – but the timing could not have been better. One of the sceptical scribes, standing with his back to the door, was just expressing his opinion of various scrolls: "This so-called Book of the Law is no more the inspired word of Yahweh than any of the other old scrolls, but at least they are all consistent," he said, "while the new scrolls...." His words tailed off as he noticed the distracted gazes and respectful responses of those of his audience who were facing the doorway.

He turned to see the reason and met the eyes of King Josiah, who looked at him enquiringly. "You were saying...?" he prompted quietly.

"Ah, it was... n-n-nothing im-important, my lord," he stammered.

The king looked at him hard for a few moments, then looked around at everyone else. He must have known that something unusual was going on, since we were all standing in a group near the centre of the room and no-one was doing any of the normal work of copying or checking.

"Hilkiah, is there any news to report?" asked Josiah. "The final check of the last two sheets was to be finished today, wasn't it? Is it all completed now?"

"Ah," said my father, unconsciously copying the earlier scribe: "There have been some... unexpected delays," he continued, looking at me. He probably agreed with the sceptical scribes that it was all my fault! And maybe it was, although I wouldn't have said that it was a fault. My father's plans for bringing me back into the fold never did work very well. As I watched my father's face, it was obvious that he was struggling to decide what to do. He had the ultimate responsibility for the work of copying the Book of the Law for King Josiah. Would Josiah be so determined to get his copy quickly that he would be willing to accept a poor quality result? What if someone suggested to Josiah that the updates were undesirable? My father looked at me again, and I felt confident that I was gauging his thought processes quite accurately; after all, my father would be sure that I was the most likely person to find a way to tell Josiah such a thing.

I could hardly breathe as my father made up his mind. This was a vitally important decision. True, if he made the wrong decision, it might still be possible to reverse it later, but this would be the easiest way to choose the right path.

"Ah…" he began again, looking down and tapping his fingers slowly on the table, and I wondered what decision he had made, or whether he was still wrestling with the answer. "The… ah… initial copies have tested the process thoroughly," he continued slowly, "and we are very satisfied with that. Ah… however," he paused, before continuing even more slowly, "some, or all, of the… ah… actual copies may need to be redone."

He had made the right decision! Or, at least, he had made the first move towards the right decision. There would now be an opportunity to make sure that the Book of the Law said what God had originally written it to say. My father's voice, normally so impressive and confident, had sounded almost old as he spoke, and a little concern tempered my joy.

Josiah looked around at the group and asked, "Does that mean I will have to wait longer to get my copy?"

Immer intervened, saying, "My lord, it may do. We are not sure yet because we are reconsidering the updating which was being done at the same time as the copying. As you will remember, we were updating some of the old-fashioned script and wording, but it appears that we may need to reconsider some of the changes."

"You are the experts," responded Josiah, "so I will wait for your decision. If a delay will give a better result, a result more true to the word of Yahweh," he paused a moment and looked pointedly at the sceptical scribe who had been expressing his doubts about inspiration before continuing, "…then the delay is worthwhile. Might it be better to make a first batch of copies that are identical to the original, with no updating or changing at all? Then updated copies could be made later once there was less need for haste."

"That is one possibility," agreed Immer. "Another similar option is to make copies in modern script, while changing nothing else. That would be easier to read, as well as being easier for the scribes to write."

"Well I definitely want to be able to read mine," said the king emphatically, "and while I find the old script intriguing, it is quite difficult to read quickly."

"Maybe that would be the easiest solution then," agreed my father, and Immer nodded too.

There was nothing else to show the king that day, and he seemed a little disappointed as he left, pausing only to encourage my father and Immer to decide as quickly as possible, but to choose the path that would get the fastest results that our God would be happy with.

⚭

Nothing more was said in public about the sceptical scribe and his expressed opinion that none of our scrolls were the work of God. However, I never heard him express that sort of opinion again, so I guess that someone must have warned him to be careful. He didn't become an advocate of Yahweh as the author of our religious texts, but at least his poison would no longer be spread so freely.

It's not hard to see why evil wins so often and why my nation has always tended towards decay. Righteous people and righteous kings are prone to show mercy and forgiveness, but evil leaders have no such tendencies, and their attacks on the righteous are merciless.

Righteousness, already a tender, fragile plant, loses much of its precious fruit in this world because of the relentless attacks of evil people. At the same time, the mercy of the righteous often allows the aggressive weed of evil to keep its abundant fruit and spread its seed even more widely.

Later, I found a consoling thought in Moses' song in the Book of the Law: Vengeance belongs to God. He will repay[55].

❧

Exhausted by my busy night and excited by the anticipation of a victory in the struggle against the attempts to "update" the Book of the Law, I was quite pleased when my father said that there was no point in me checking the one remaining sheet. The review committee would have to meet again urgently to make a "final" decision regarding the updates.

My father and Immer were cautious in their words, but both seemed resigned to the fact that all sixteen sheets would need to be copied again. Not only that, but Josiah had made it clear that he would prefer copies made with very limited changes, as this would speed up the process. Even so, there would be a delay of at least six days, and the king would not be pleased.

Not long after King Josiah's departure, my father and Immer also left to convene yet another meeting of the review committee.

For a short time, I considered leaving for Anathoth immediately, but the attraction of the Book of the Law was too great. I still did not know most of its contents and could not pass up the opportunity to read as much of it as possible – even with its discredited updates.

No-one else had any immediate interest in the copied sheets, so I sat down at the table where they were stacked.

---

[55] Deuteronomy 32:35, 41

Taking the first, I began to read the starting passage of the book, the passage my father had first read out to an audience of Levites when his curiosity had unearthed the Book of the Law in the temple.

I had read about two thirds of the first sheet when this long day delivered yet another surprise: Shaphan the king's secretary entered the room. Observing that neither my father nor Immer was present, he asked where they were. I answered that they were arranging a meeting, or maybe in the middle of it.

"Do you know where their meeting would be?" he asked. "King Josiah has an important question to ask them."

"I'm sorry, but I don't," I replied, before asking everyone else in the room, "Does anyone know where the review committee could be meeting?"

A chorus of negative answers arose.

"That's a pity," said Shaphan. "King Josiah has ordered the leaders from all of the towns of Judah to come to Jerusalem so that he can inform them about the discovery of the Book of the Law. They are to arrive in five days, and the king had planned to read the book to them. With this latest delay in copying, he wants to know what will be available to be read to the leaders."

The scribes and Validators looked at each other, and some of the more senior scribes began to suggest that it might be best to wait until the copies had been completed. Shaphan looked displeased with these suggestions, and I guessed that Josiah had made it perfectly clear that waiting was not an acceptable option.

My earlier idea of reading the Book of the Law to all of the people resurfaced in my mind, and I blurted out, "Why not delay the reading of the Book of the Law for a little while and then read it out to all of the people, not just the leaders?"

Shaphan looked at me thoughtfully and replied, "That might be a good thought, Jeremiah. I shall mention it to the king. He is chafing at any delay in spreading abroad the words of the Book of the Law, and this suggestion may well be to his liking." He gave an inclusive nod of farewell to all in the room and hurried out.

I returned to my own reading of the Book of the Law, but a picture of a large crowd thronging the courtyard of the temple as they listened to the king reading God's words kept intruding. Silent words of thankful prayer filled my mind. Yahweh would not allow me to pray for my people, but at least I could thank him for his work in giving Josiah opportunities. How I hoped that Josiah would take this opportunity! And how I longed for the freedom to pray....

By the time my father and I left for Anathoth that evening, several important decisions had been made. With God's help, the victory had been won, but the events took some time – which was a little worrying.

The review committee finally decided to update the Book of the Law with a very light hand indeed: modern script, modern abbreviations and modern spelling would be used, but no other changes would be made.

When my father reported this decision to the scribes and Validators, I rejoiced, although I believed that it would probably leave some parts of the text quite hard to understand. Meshullam and I discussed the decision afterwards and concluded that it was the best possible option. The making of the first updated copy would progress more easily, so that the Book of the Law would be available more quickly. Not only that, but further updating could still follow, with the advantage that there would be many copies of the original wording available for verification. Words and ideas could not be changed without it being known that the modifications had occurred.

From the snippets I heard of other conversations around the room, it seemed that most agreed this was the best solution, although a few were militantly against leaving the job "half done", as they put it. These hard-liners saw no advantage in having copies of the Book of the Law that used modern script and spelling, while some clearly expressed their displeasure at the idea of copies being available which had not been censored to remove the "old-fashioned bigoted nonsense". I took careful note of who these people were: it seemed likely that we would come into conflict at some point in the future.

Before we had concluded our discussions, Shaphan returned and called my father and Immer to an urgent meeting with the king. Events were moving rapidly, and the effects of the Book of the Law might be able to spread more widely and quickly than had been expected.

It was hard to sit and wait. Time passed and still they did not return, and I began to be a little concerned as the darkening shadows proclaimed the arrival of evening. One by one, the scribes and Validators left, until I was left alone, fighting sleep and trying to concentrate on my reading in the wavering light of a single lamp. The natural light from the elevated windows was fading fast and the light of the lamp now held sway in the empty room. Utter darkness would surely overtake us before we reached Anathoth.

Just as the sun set, they returned. I hastily put away the copied sheets I had been reading, and my father and I left immediately. There was no time for any discussion, and it was quite dark by the time we had left the city and climbed to the saddle between Har Hatsophim and the Mount of Olives. As usual, my father was short of breath after the climb, and we were walking quite slowly. We were both very familiar with the path, but a familiarity in daylight is quite different from what is needed to walk in the dark with only the light of half a moon for guidance. I was concerned for my father, given his increasing caution when walking which had already caught my attention.

Our progress was slow as we walked along the hillside path towards Anathoth, and my father was able to tell me the outcome of his meeting with King Josiah. The king had decided to summon all the people of Judah immediately. The meeting with the leaders would still take place on the eleventh day of the month as planned, but a gathering of all of the people would be called for the fourteenth of the month. Every man in Judah was to be invited to the capital to hear the words of the Book of the Law of Yahweh just seven days from now. The king hoped that Jerusalem would be filled from end to end with people eager to hear the long-lost words of God.

Passing through the small grove of trees, now with its mixed memories, the path was shaded and very dark in places. As we were about to emerge from under the shadowing trees, my father suddenly stumbled, cried out and fell to the ground by the side of the path. I was walking very close behind him, but could do nothing to prevent or soften his fall.

Before I had even reached him, my father was already trying to stand up, and at first he refused my offered hand. However, when he tried to put some weight on his left foot, a sharp pain caused him to quickly grab my hand, catching me by surprise and almost making me fall over too. However, I was able to regain my balance and give him the support he needed. His left ankle seemed to be badly twisted, and for a time it could not carry any weight at all. We sat for a few minutes in the darkness, and as we did so, he began to notice the extra cuts and bruises he had suffered in his fall. The night was not at all cold, so I knew that there would be no dangers from the weather, but I also knew that my mother would be wondering where we were. I was about to suggest that I should go and fetch some help from Anathoth when my father began to struggle to his feet.

"Hold my hand again," I said, and he did so, grasping it firmly.

"It feels a little better now," he said, and started to climb back onto the path. "Let's see how well I can walk."

Slowly and carefully, we climbed back onto the path and began to walk towards Anathoth again. Once we had emerged from the shadow of the trees, the steady light of the moon made it much easier to choose our footing. Sudden intakes of breath and a tightening of the grip on my arm showed that my father's ankle was still painful, but he managed to keep walking gingerly along the uneven path.

I was glad to be there to help, but I also hoped that the incident might soften my father's attitude toward me and my work. Whether it did or not, I can't really say, but I didn't have any more confrontations with my father for a while afterwards, so maybe it did.

Limping slowly and cautiously in the darkness, my father made his way determinedly to our house, leaning increasingly heavily on my arm. My mother was watching for us, having done her best to make sure that the meal would not burn. As my father made his way inside, my mother fussed over him like a cow with a newborn calf. Within moments, he was lying on a bed with his ankle being soothed and cleansed with water. A few more moments, and healing creams and comforting bandages were being applied and my mother was administering some warming broth from a wooden bowl. My father would certainly not suffer for want of care!

But as I watched, I wondered: would his injury have any effect on the plans for the copying and reading of the Book of the Law?

Chapter 13

Come to Jerusalem!

Josiah's reign was long and godly, yet his best, most expansive work for God was done in just a few isolated weeks – short periods of time that accomplished a huge amount with God's help. Yet, in the end, his reign made very little difference to the nation overall.

The command that all leaders should come to Jerusalem to hear an explanation of the horrifying curses in the Book of the Law, and the invitation for everyone in Judah to come and listen to the reading of the entire book, were seismic events. Not only did Josiah want everyone to hear the message and understand his determination to effect change, but he was already developing some plans for events that would follow.

I went to the city early in the morning on the seventh day of the month, the morning after my father had twisted his ankle, to report his injury and to see whether I could finish reading the Book of the Law for myself.

When I arrived in the scroll room that day, Shaphan was talking to Immer. They were obviously making plans for finalising the copy of the Book of the Law that would be read. Copying the Book of the Law was about to recommence after the conflict over the so-called "updates", and it was decided that the first set of sheets produced would be used to make the reading as easy as possible. The only drawback would be that each sheet would have been written by a different scribe, each with slightly different handwriting – it would never be sewn together as a final scroll in that way, because of the cosmetic appearance. As I entered, Immer called me over to ask where my father was. Apparently, Josiah wanted my father to be the one to read the Book of the Law to the people, with his powerful and delightful voice. However, Josiah had also made it clear to Shaphan that if anything made this impossible, he would not consider delaying the reading in any way. It must happen on the day planned, and if my father could not read it, Josiah would read it himself.

On hearing of my father's injury, Shaphan and Immer discussed the matter, and concluded that Josiah would probably not be happy with my father leading the reading unless he was able to come for the practice that had been arranged for the twelfth day of the month, two days before the planned gathering. I was asked to pass on these details to my father, and did so that evening. While my father was extremely gratified that the king wanted him to read the Book of the Law, he was not sure whether he would be able to get to the temple on the appointed day. My father had been able to walk home the night before when he had twisted his ankle, but since that time, he had been unable even to put his foot on the floor.

Meanwhile, as the copying of the new set of sheets went on around me, I read the original copied and modified sheets, which nobody really wanted any more because the updates did not have the support of the king. Only time would tell, but I was hoping that if I walked a careful path, I might be able to keep those sheets myself. If so, I planned to destroy them. False words are so very dangerous. And the closer they are to truth, the more dangerous they are. Having now read about half of the copied sheets and checked some of them against the original sheets, I began to feel that I was able to identify many places where the words had been changed to "modernise" them. By the end of that day, I had read through the copied version completely three times, and been able to check many of the places where I was suspicious that the word of God had been modified. I had also received permission from Immer to make notes about these changes on the sheets themselves. As part of my plan to get these unwanted sheets for myself, I was eager to begin marking them myself. Immer seemed to be in a better mood than I had ever known him to be. No doubt the general excitement in the city, and his own important part in it, encouraged him.

ℭЯ

By the tenth day of the month, the day before the meeting of the leaders, each of the scribes had completed his copy of the first sheet, and the validation had begun. I had expected to take part in the validation, but the father of the Validator I had replaced had made an amazing recovery, and the Validator had returned to Jerusalem, eager to continue the work that would be so important to his future career. I was no longer needed, which left me free to spend my time declaring the words of God to the people as they entered the temple.

The message had proved unpopular, and things might have turned out unpleasantly for me if King Josiah had not been in power. Many people took offence at the condemnation of the adoration of other gods, while many others became angry when I spoke of God rejecting the worship of any who came to the temple with no intention of changing their sinful behaviour. However, what surprised me most was the large number of people who objected to God's threats to destroy the temple as he had the place of worship in Shiloh. This large group of worshippers seemed to find that threat more upsetting than any of God's other words. Not only so, but since many either did not believe that these were the words of Yahweh or did not believe that Yahweh could ever feel like that, their anger was directed at the messenger – me.

Azariah had come to listen to the message once that day, but he had never talked to me about it. However, he had obviously mentioned it to my father, because my father called me over during the evening and asked me to repeat the words to him. After only a few sentences, my father almost exploded as I related God's words:

> " 'Do not trust in these deceptive words:
> "This is the temple of the Lord,
> the temple of the Lord,
> the temple of the Lord." '[56]"

However, he controlled himself enough to be able to ask in a relatively mild voice, "In what way are those words deceptive, my son?"

"What if Yahweh chooses to leave this temple?" I replied, answering with a question. "People seem to feel that the temple is an everlasting symbol of God's approval, a sort of talisman that gives us protection as a nation; but Yahweh left his house in Shiloh. God wants us to realise that the temple is no protection for us if we are not obedient."

---

[56] Jeremiah 7:4

My father did not respond, but his lips remained tightly pursed as I continued with the rest of the words of God. I suspect that he could not even begin to consider the possibility that God might abandon his temple.

$$\text{\it CR}$$

My father had, of course, been invited to the meeting of leaders, but his damaged ankle had prevented him from attending. Instead, my brother Azariah had gone along as his representative, and I was present that evening when he visited to report what had happened.

About a thousand leaders had attended and the open square in front of the king's palace had been filled with men. A wooden platform[57] had been built so that all would be able to see the king and his helpers during the event.

The eighth month is the start of our rainy season, but the rain generally begins slowly, with only a few days of rain in the eighth month. Josiah began his welcome to the leaders in clear sunshine, with an acknowledgement of the blessings of Yahweh, as could be seen in such benign weather. Azariah described the platform with its trappings of royal purple and blue. The box in which the Book of the Law had been found stood on the platform throughout the day.

Josiah had intended my father to describe the discovery of the Book of the Law, and I imagined how it would have been with my father's rich voice retelling the enthralling story while the original wrappings of the scroll were displayed to the fascinated throng. However, as my

---

[57] Solomon built a bronze platform 3 cubits (1.5 metres or 4.5 feet) high for the dedication of the temple (2 Chronicles 6:13), and in the time of Nehemiah, Ezra and others stood on a wooden platform so that all the people could see them (Nehemiah 8:4).

father's ankle injury had prevented this, Azariah had told the story instead. Next, Immer had reported the progress made in copying the book and then Josiah had spoken to the leaders, stressing the blessings of Yahweh in bringing Israel out of Egypt, and destroying the nations which had lived in Canaan before us. But he had also had Shaphan read the sections of both blessings and curses from the Book of the Law[58].

Azariah had been impressed by Shaphan's reading from the Book of the Law and the amount of preparation that had obviously been put into organising the whole day. His involvement had been minimal, but he had been very pleased to join in the work of reformation which King Josiah was promoting. It would be good, he thought, for the people of Judah to worship Yahweh more, making sure that all the correct rituals were observed.

I didn't bother asking, but I wondered just how much Azariah had read of the Book of the Law himself and how much he knew of the contents of the scrolls that I had been reading recently in our scroll room. After my father had hurt his ankle, I had continued to read more of the scrolls he had shown to me, doing a lot of reading, and getting very little sleep. I had read scrolls that told of creation, of Noah, Abraham, Isaac and Jacob. Others too, ancient scrolls that told of the events in the wilderness as God led Israel out of Egypt into the land in which we now lived. When Azariah spoke of rituals, how much had he read of the rituals himself in the words of Moses?

I also heard more details the next day from Shallum, Huldah's husband, who had been present to attend King Josiah and make sure that he was splendidly presented as usual. You might think that a serious young man like Josiah should be able to manage his clothes by himself, and, of course, most of the time you would be right.

---

[58] Deuteronomy 27 & 28

Shallum was there for the situations when a busy king needed someone else to make absolutely sure that his clothing was impeccably presented, and that no unexpected or embarrassing mistakes could be made.

Shallum told me that Josiah had watched the crowd carefully while Shaphan was reading the promised blessings and curses. He guessed that Josiah would have been pleased that some of the leaders had seemed to respond in much the same way as Josiah himself had done when he had heard the curses. But, continued Shallum, it was only a very few. Most had listened to Shaphan with interest as he had read from two of the copied sheets, but had showed none of the horror and abject humility felt by their king.

Apparently even Benaiah the son of Kenan from Anathoth had been there, attending at the king's command and doing his best to look as if he favoured Josiah's goals of religious reform. I had not seen him since his failed attempt to have me beaten for destroying the idol on the hillside opposite Anathoth. However, the work to enlarge the shrine had continued, and I wondered whether this work would be affected by Josiah's meeting with the leaders.

One theme which Josiah had apparently brought up time after time through the day was the upcoming reading of the Book of the Law, which was to happen in only three days' time. Several times he had urged all of the leaders to attend, while veiled hints had suggested that any who did not attend might not be considered qualified to lead any more in Judah. Shallum reported to me that many of the leaders from further afield had decided to stay in Jerusalem until the fourteenth day of the month, staying with relatives in the city if they had any, or simply camping out in the square near the king's gate if they had no other choice. Some who lived closer were hurrying back to their towns to encourage others to come to

Jerusalem to hear the Book of the Law, and join the king's reformation.

❧

The two days leading up to the special reading of the Book of the Law were very busy days in Jerusalem. The temple precinct was filled with people making sure that as much room as possible would be available for those who were coming to listen, while others started to build another, slightly larger, wooden platform from which the book would be read to all the people. Workers swarmed over the buildings, trying to roll back the centuries and present Yahweh's temple as clean and new again.

My father's ankle was recovering slowly, but when the preparation for reading the Book of the Law took place, he was not able to be in Jerusalem. Instead, King Josiah would read the text to his nation.

Jerusalem itself was abuzz with excitement and a thousand people were called to help with preparations throughout the city, while many families were also preparing their houses for visits by relatives who would come from all corners of the country.

Many units of the army were called to Jerusalem, partly to provide added support and security, but also because King Josiah wanted his soldiers to know more about the God they all should worship.

❧

This reading of the Book of the Law and the events that surrounded it were of supreme importance for the nation. Many would come simply because it was a special event, but I felt that it would also be good for people to feel the strength of faith amongst those who loved God's law.

We had received news at home that several members of my mother's family were coming to Jerusalem to hear the Book of the Law. They would be going directly to the temple, but would like a place to stay for a few days afterwards. My father and mother had naturally invited them to stay at our house, so it would be pleasantly crowded again for a while. I tried hard to convince my mother to come to Jerusalem to hear the words of God, and was very pleased when she agreed despite her strong opinions about preparing thoroughly for visitors.

I sought out my three particular childhood friends and encouraged them to attend. Benaiah refused and Chelub followed his lead. Adaiah said that he would think about it.

Hanamel, my cousin, was also on my list of people who should be encouraged to come. He was living in Anathoth again now, and spent much of his time learning the duties assigned to the tribe of Levi. Sadly, this would not include reading the Book of the Law, but at least he could go and listen to it being read. He, too, told me that he would think about it, and I reminded him that God had written these words for his nation, so if he wanted to be part of God's nation, he should take the opportunity to go and listen.

ℂℛ

As the afternoon drew to a close on the thirteenth day of the month, the temple courts were finally ready for the reading of the Book of the Law. The wooden platform had been completed and stood with splendid decoration, nestling against the southernmost of the two enormous pillars at the front of the temple building. According to custom, this was the king's position in the temple[59], and it

---

[59] 2 Chronicles 23:13; 2 Kings 23:3; 2 Chronicles 34:31

was from here that the people would hear the word of Yahweh read.

All of the cleaning of the temple courts had been finished and the dust and rubbish had been removed. From a physical point of view at least, the temple was cleansed, ready to receive the very large crowds that were expected on the exciting morning that would follow.

The evening sun set on a city that was breathlessly expectant. I continued to pray that all the planning and hard work would pay off. Cautiously, I prayed that this would be the spark which started a raging fire of reformation such as the country had never seen before. I was still getting used to God's commandment that I should not pray for my people, and sometimes it was difficult to know where to stop – what would be allowed and what would not. Probably I crossed the line at times, but it was hard not to.

☙

The morning of the fourteenth dawned fine and clear, and I enjoyed the calming presence of the living God while watching the beauty of both moonset and sunrise from my accustomed hillside. At first the tentative light in the east had little effect on the vista, lit as it was by the moon as it sank in the west. But the light from the east gradually spread as the sun readied itself for the day's work of spreading God's light over his creation. I was up earlier than usual, as I needed to arrive in Jerusalem as early as possible. But first, the foundation of the day must be laid in the strength and peace of the presence of God. Today, King Josiah's demand for reformation would be made on behalf of God; it would be a day of joy and solemn warning for the whole nation.

It promised to be a day such as the kingdom of Judah had never seen before. A day when Yahweh was proclaimed above all other gods, and idols would be publicly ridiculed.

After a time of communion and peace in the growing light, I returned to the house just before the sun edged its way above the horizon. The work of Yahweh was calling me.

Our entire family was going to Jerusalem that day. My father felt that his ankle had improved sufficiently to allow him to make the trip, and my mother and Gemariah would walk with him and provide any help he needed.

Azariah was already in Jerusalem, representing my father with the assistance of the priests of the second order. These were priests who were chosen mostly for their organisational skills, and did much of the work of maintaining the orderly operation of the temple. My father was nominally their boss, but they did most of the ongoing supervision of temple operations. Azariah would take their advice as he learned the responsibilities of the position that he would later assume as High Priest. My father's injury had given Azariah an opportunity to experience the power of the position of High Priest; I hoped it would light a flame of serious godliness in him so that he would be equipped to be the spiritual leader that a High Priest ought to be.

Shortly after sunrise I was walking toward Jerusalem carrying some food for the day, as well as some to eat on the way. Again I passed the shrine that was under construction in the grove. Josiah's commands and entreaties at the leaders' meeting in Jerusalem did not seem to have slowed the progress of this hideous sign of idolatry. Instead, solid walls had been constructed, and paintings of imagined scenes had been added to the rear wall, glorifying the imagined, but childish, behaviour of their foolish images. Anger rose in me, but there was no time to do anything about it then, so I hurried on towards Jerusalem.

Jerusalem came into view as I crested the saddle between Har Hatsophim and the Mount of Olives. The early morning sun shone low over the Mount of Olives and painted the tawny walls of the city a deep golden hue. The temple gleamed with burnished bronze, and its newly cleaned stonework glowed as it stood alone in its position above the city. It was a picture of lyric beauty as the city of peace lay in peace below me.

I tore myself away from the view and hurried into the city to join the crowd of those who had come early to the temple. Most were people eager to hear the Book of the Law, having come from near and far at the invitation of their king. My task was to speak to them the words that God had given me, words for those who came to worship.

With a large and growing crowd to speak to, I looked for a place to stand. Today, the low walls near the temple gates which I had recently been using were all covered with people waiting for the day's activities to start. The piles of building materials had all been cleared away for this special day, and no carts were delivering any more. But there was one cart standing near the gate, and I walked towards it, hoping to be able to take advantage of its height as I shouted God's message to the people.

Then suddenly I recognised the cart, and a flash of understanding came to me. This was the very cart I had seen when speaking to the people in the thirteenth year of Josiah: a cart loaded with fleeces and dye. On this morning there were some rolls of flaxen thread as well. More than four years ago, I had stood on this very cart to make God's message easier to hear, and now I knew exactly where the goods were going: the wool, flax and dye were all going to the room where that woman was. Goods for such evil purposes were being delivered to that place even as the final preparations were being made for reading from the Book of the Law of God. The deliveries had probably even been arranged early to ensure that the horrible work could continue while the great gathering was underway! Thousands of people would be gathered in the temple courts to hear God's word, while at the same time hangings for the worship of Asherah would continue to be made in that room, deep in the temple of Yahweh!

For a time I was speechless with fury. How could the nation ever be made holy while this undermining of the king's goals continued? And how could this weaving business continue unless those who visited Yahweh's temple were doing so with the intention of worshipping Asherah and Baal and all the host of heaven? Once again, I began to feel the light and fire of God's word, and the words that God had given me to deliver flamed into white-hot brilliance in my mind. But once again, the words were augmented with pictures, this time in the form of a guided vision. I turned toward the gate of the temple and saw the horses standing on either side of the gate. They had been there for as long as I had known the temple, but suddenly I really looked at them. It's hard to understand, really, but when you are familiar with things, used to seeing them around, they do not always have the impact on you that they should. You probably have the same difficulty too – if you stop and look carefully around your own town you may be surprised just how many items of worship to false gods there are around. When we are familiar with such things, they can simply blend into the scenery so that we do not notice them as we should.

But with God's help, I was now seeing clearly. No longer did I see a decorative post at each side of the gateway: instead, I saw horses dedicated to the sun[60], with the sun and its rays shaped into the cast metal. Each stood

---

[60] 2 Kings 23:11

on a pedestal, and wooden chariots were artistically arranged on the pavement beside them, with the rayed sun painted on their sides.

Beyond the gateway, in the court that was slowly filling with people, my newly-opened eyes saw an altar[61] with carvings representing stars and other objects in the heavens. And as I saw these hideous contradictions in the temple of Yahweh, the sayings of Yahweh that shone blindingly brightly in my mind were the words:

> "Do not trust in these deceptive words:
> 'This is the temple of the Lord,
> the temple of the Lord,
> the temple of the Lord.' "[62]

Was this really the temple of Yahweh at all? This seemed to be the question that God was asking me. Can it really be a temple of Yahweh when symbols forbidden by God greet worshippers at the gate, encouraging the adoration of other gods and directly breaking more of God's commands? My mind's eyes were led elsewhere in the temple and I saw an Asherah pole[63], intricately carved and skilfully painted, surrounded by the paraphernalia used in the worship of Asherah[64]. Then the scene changed, and once again I was inside the room where that woman plied her trade, and God made me see the true uses of that building that broke so many more of his laws[65].

I had come to speak God's words to the people, but instead, God had made me see the reasons for those words more clearly than ever. What should I do now? The words of God were still burning painfully brightly within

---

[61] 2 Kings 21:5; 23:12

[62] Jeremiah 7:4

[63] 2 Kings 23:6

[64] 2 Kings 23:4

[65] 2 Kings 23:7

me, and the urge to do God's work was stronger than ever. Immediately the knowledge came that the work he wanted me to do was to repeat his words to the worshippers who were passing through the gates of the temple. So I stood and shouted the words of God to the people again and again as the crowd built up in the temple court and near the gates.

It was as I was finishing the message for the sixth or seventh time that I saw some of the nobles of Judah walking toward me from the lower parts of the city. Maaseiah, now promoted to the position of governor of Jerusalem[66], was in the lead, and when he heard my words, he came right up to me. He looked far from pleased as I finished with the words:

> " 'And I will silence in the cities of Judah
> and in the streets of Jerusalem
> the voice of mirth and the voice of gladness,
> the voice of the bridegroom and the voice of the bride,
> for the land shall become a waste.'[67]"

"Still no good news, Jeremiah?" he began. "How can you keep saying such depressing things on a day like this? King Josiah is presenting the Book of the Law to all the people to encourage the worship of God, and you continue to give a message of disaster and destruction. How can that help the king with his work of reform?"

I could understand his feelings – as governor of a city that God was planning to destroy! But God's words must be delivered, and they would never be complimentary when Judah was ignoring him.

"You heard the curses that God announced in the wilderness when you heard the Book of the Law," I

---

66 2 Chronicles 34:8
67 Jeremiah 7:34

replied. "Yahweh keeps his word, but we, his people, have not."

"I'm not going to get involved in an argument with you here, young man," Maaseiah snapped. "All I want from you is an assurance that you will not interfere with the king's plans for today. His program includes the reading of the Book of the Law and several other important activities. The king will be arriving very soon through his gate from the palace, and soldiers will be around to make sure that no-one causes trouble. Unless you can give me such an assurance now, you will be taken into custody immediately. Nothing can be allowed to interrupt the program today." He looked at me sternly and gestured towards a squad of soldiers just taking their place at the gates, while another marched up from the lower city. "What is your choice, Jeremiah?"

"I was to speak the words of God until King Josiah's program was ready to begin," I stated. "If the program is about to begin, I am happy to finish now." I had been surprised by the direct threat from Maaseiah, but it made sense, and I did not want to cause any trouble to King Josiah on this very special day. However, I remember wondering to myself what would happen if God suddenly wanted me to deliver a message from him in the middle of the reading of the Book of the Law. My intention would not matter if God's intention was otherwise.... Maaseiah took my answer to be the assurance he was looking for. "Good," he said, and strode off with the other nobles towards the group of soldiers at the gate.

Excitedly, I joined the lines of people still streaming into the temple, and was swallowed up in the teeming mass of people who were all doing their best to find places where they would be able to see and hear King Josiah.

I was still trying to find a place where I could see the platform when a stir went through the crowd and people began to turn and crane their necks towards the south side of the temple courts where a special gate led from the king's palace.

Josiah, surrounded by his nobles and an escort of guards, was making his way towards the wooden platform.

Chapter 14

So much to do!

A wooden platform large enough for a dozen men to stand on nestled against the massive bronze pillar in front of the vestibule of the temple. It was decorated with linen hangings embroidered with gold, blue, purple and scarlet threads. In front of the platform and on either side, was a huge crowd of people, some sitting and some standing. Both courts of the temple were full to overflowing with people who had gathered from the cities, towns and countryside of Judah to celebrate the discovery of the Book of the Law of Yahweh. Everyone was ready to rejoice, and before the day was out, they would all have heard the will of God more clearly than they had ever done before in their life. Many would consider again the nation's commitment to the God who had led their fathers out of Egypt and into this land flowing with milk and honey. How would they respond?

King Josiah climbed onto the platform and stood above the crowd in the king's place next to the pillar named Jachin[68]. When all the people saw him raise his arms to the crowd in smiling greeting, there were scattered spontaneous cheers which spread and grew until the whole assembly was welcoming and cheering their king for several minutes, and the shouts of the people were heard from far away.

After some time, the noise began to abate, and King Josiah welcomed the crowd. The throng became hushed and everyone strained to hear the strong, pleasant voice of their handsome young king. People from one end of the land to the other were gathered together in a way that had not happened for many years, and excitement and joy spread through the whole crowd as they rejoiced in fellowship within the courts of Yahweh's temple. Those still arriving met the multitude well before they reached the gates of the temple, and large numbers of people were caught in the press outside the Benjamin Gate of the city and missed the serious but encouraging words of Josiah.

King Josiah spoke of the parlous state of religion in Judah and how the providential discovery of the Book of the Law of Yahweh had given us all, as a nation, an opportunity to return to God in a meaningful way.

Once again, the box in which my father had found the scroll was sitting on the platform. I could see my father sitting near the platform, but he looked exhausted after his walk from Anathoth, and again it was Azariah who told the story of the discovery of the Book of the Law in the crowded temple storeroom. For many, this story was new, and the crowd hung on his every word; a collective sigh was heard when the ancient scroll was finally freed from

---

[68] 2 Chronicles 23:13 does not indicate what the pillar was that Josiah stood beside, nor does 2 Kings 23:3 with Joash. It seems likely to have been one of the two enormous bronze pillars at the entrance to the temple. Jachin was the one on the south (1 Kings 7:21), so it was on the right hand side as one faced out of the temple.

its hiding place of many years. The cleverly carved wooden section that had hidden the scroll was held aloft with the wrappings as Azariah told of our father's careful unwrapping of the ancient scroll. Finally, the individual sheets of the scroll were shown as well. Azariah concluded with the statement that the experts among the priests and scribes were convinced that this scroll was genuinely very old and equally genuinely a record of the words of Yahweh, spoken through Moses about nine hundred years before, as the nation had prepared to enter the land of Canaan.

King Josiah then described his feelings when Shaphan had read the scroll to him. He expressed his amazement at hearing the laws of Yahweh as he had never heard them before, and his horror at Yahweh's utter condemnation of the sorts of behaviour that he, King Josiah, had considered normal all his life. Josiah briefly described some of the curses which Yahweh had pronounced against his nation if they did not keep his commandments, and tried to convey the feelings of guilt and terror which had overwhelmed him. He made no attempt to hide any of these feelings, but instead described how he had sent representatives to visit Huldah the prophetess because of the shame and fear which had prevented him from lifting up his face before God.

The crowd listened to this narrative in an amazed silence, and many a man looked at his neighbour to confirm that he was hearing the words correctly. The king! Their righteous king, a dedicated worshipper of Yahweh, ashamed and terrified, too full of guilt and fear to visit the prophetess personally? As the king finished, there was much exchanging of confused looks and shuffling of feet as his audience tried to comprehend the significance of this narrative.

Shaphan spoke next, describing the visit to Huldah, and reading out the answer from God which she had conveyed. He highlighted God's approval of King Josiah because of his humility and emphasised that, maybe, if the nation as a whole responded in the same way, peace could be found in our time through service to God.

Josiah had included these introductory details to prepare the people for what they were to hear and to indicate what their response should be if they wanted to please Yahweh. Once Shaphan had finished, Josiah stepped forward again. It was time to read the Book of the Law, but the king felt that a prayer to God was needed first. King Josiah prayed to Yahweh on behalf of his people, praying that God would give the blessings of wisdom and understanding to all who had come. He prayed that all would be able to hear clearly and that what they heard would touch their hearts and inspire obedience in each heart.

Several elders among the priests and Levites stood on the platform with the king, ready to explain the words of the Book of the Law as they were read[69]. Of course, most of them had very little knowledge of what the book contained because its discovery had been so recent. If allowed free rein, their interpretations would probably have eased the pain caused by God's uncompromising laws and judgements, but they would not be allowed much time and there was no need for explanation where the text was very clear.

After a brief explanation of the historical context of these words written at the end of Moses' life, King Josiah began to read in a powerful voice:

> " 'These are the words that Moses spoke to all Israel
> beyond the Jordan in the wilderness,
> in the Arabah opposite Suph,

---

[69] Nehemiah 8:4-8 describes a later reading of the Book of the Law. Levites helped with reading and explaining the meaning.

between Paran and Tophel, Laban,
Hazeroth, and Dizahab.
It is eleven days' journey from Horeb
by the way of Mount Seir to Kadesh-barnea.
In the fortieth year,
on the first day of the eleventh month,
Moses spoke to the people of Israel according to all
that the Lord had given him
in commandment to them.'[70]"

Josiah continued to read, stopping every so often for one or more of the elders to make some comments about what had just been read. King Josiah's voice was strong and clear as he read[71] of the wilderness wanderings; of the ten commandments; of Yahweh as the one and only god; of Yahweh's anger over the golden calf; of God's choice of the nation, not because of their righteousness, but because of his love for their ancestors; of God's help to conquer the land being given because the people of the land were so evil; of the place which God would choose as a place to put his name; of Yahweh's repeated warnings against idolatry and any following of the ways of the nations who were to be driven out before Israel; of offerings, tithes and feasts; of morality, cleanness and uncleanness; of inheritances; of a covenant with blessings and curses; of a choice between life and death, obedience and disobedience that each Israelite must make; of the specified reading of the law to all the people; of the song of Moses; and of his final blessing of the nation. Some small sections were read more than once because Josiah considered them particularly important or moving. It was almost noon by the time the reading was complete.

As had been seen before whenever the Book of the Law was heard, the responses of the listeners varied

---

[70] Deuteronomy 1:1-3
[71] 2 Kings 23:2; 2 Chronicles 34:30

widely. Some heard words which condemned and were cut to the heart, weeping as they recognised their failure to obey the commands of Yahweh. Others heard the words of promised blessings and cheered. Still others felt that certain passages were specific messages from God for them at this particular time in their lives. Most, however, listened quietly and kept their reflections between themselves and their creator.

King Josiah, his voice now sounding a little gruff from overuse, announced to the crowd that there would be a break in the proceedings. He encouraged them to spend the time in prayer to Yahweh and discussion with their neighbours about the words they had heard. In particular, he asked them to consider the covenant Yahweh had made with our fathers, a covenant we had inherited, but which Josiah wanted confirmed and renewed. Josiah took one of the sheets containing a section he had obviously chosen beforehand. "Listen to what Yahweh said through Moses, and now says to you:

" 'For you are a people holy to the Lord your God. The Lord your God has chosen you to be a people for his treasured possession, out of all the peoples who are on the face of the earth. It was not because you were more in number than any other people that the Lord set his love on you and chose you, for you were the fewest of all peoples, but it is because the Lord loves you and is keeping the oath that he swore to your fathers, that the Lord has brought you out with a mighty hand and redeemed you from the house of slavery, from the hand of Pharaoh king of Egypt. Know therefore that the Lord your God is God, the faithful God who keeps covenant and steadfast love with those who love him and keep his commandments, to a thousand generations, and repays to their face those who hate him, by destroying them. He will not be slack with one who hates him. He will repay him to his face. You shall therefore be careful to do the commandment and the statutes and the rules that I command you today.'[72] "

Josiah stopped and looked around at the crowd. "These words are written for you too," he repeated. "God has blessed us and we are his treasured possession. But are we keeping our side of the covenant? We have not been doing so as we ought, and I am determined that we shall begin to do so as a nation. Please think it over carefully."

A hush followed the king's words, and it continued as he turned away and left the platform, followed by the priests and Levites who had helped to explain the law. After a few moments though, the noise and bustle of a large group of people began to grow, and soon it was hard to believe that this multitude had stayed still and quiet for several hours.

Small groups of people remained in their places, and some could be seen deep in prayer as they acted on the king's request and the desires of their own hearts. Others tried to catch up on the time wasted in silence by speaking loud and long. But it was noticeable that the crowd did largely follow the request of the king: the discussions were mostly centred around the words of God and the covenant between God and his people. And the overwhelming response was that everyone wanted to renew the covenant. They wanted to strengthen their association with Abraham, Isaac and Jacob, with Moses and Aaron, Joshua and Caleb.

After a time, a choir of Levites moved to the foot of the platform and the melodious words of the Psalms

---

[72] Deuteronomy 7:6-11

sounded across the courtyards. The psalm had obviously been chosen for the occasion:

" 'Seek the Lord and his strength;
seek his presence continually!
Remember the wondrous works that he has done,
his miracles, and the judgments he uttered,
O offspring of Abraham, his servant,
children of Jacob, his chosen ones!
He is the Lord our God;
his judgments are in all the earth.
He remembers his covenant forever,
the word that he commanded,
for a thousand generations,
the covenant that he made with Abraham,
his sworn promise to Isaac,
which he confirmed to Jacob as a statute,
to Israel as an everlasting covenant,
saying, 'To you I will give the land of Canaan
as your portion for an inheritance.'[73]"

As the choir sang, King Josiah returned to the platform, and now he stood there alone. He was making an appeal to his nation as the king; their leader, but not their master. The choir finished their song and an expectant hush fell over the crowd. Josiah raised his arms as if to embrace the entire crowd and speak to each person individually.

"My brothers," he began, and the silence in the throng grew even deeper, "we have heard the words of the Book of the Law of Yahweh our God. His words have instructed, commanded, demanded and reminded. Our fathers made a covenant with Yahweh at Mount Sinai, and again as they were about to enter this land in which

---

[73] Psalm 105:4-11

we now live.   Remember the words you heard this morning:

" 'You are standing today all of you before the Lord your God: the heads of your tribes, your elders, and your officers, all the men of Israel, your little ones, your wives, and the sojourner who is in your camp, from the one who chops your wood to the one who draws your water, so that you may enter into the sworn covenant of the Lord your God, which the Lord your God is making with you today, that he may establish you today as his people, and that he may be your God, as he promised you, and as he swore to your fathers, to Abraham, to Isaac, and to Jacob. It is not with you alone that I am making this sworn covenant, but with whoever is standing here with us today before the Lord our God, and with whoever is not here with us today.'[74]"

"We are among those who were not present with Moses, but are still obligated to keep this covenant. We have not done so, and have the curses of God hanging over us. Be sure that they will come upon us unless we repent.

"You have all heard the commandments; you have heard the promised blessings and curses. What do you want? Are you willing to renew the covenant and walk with Yahweh our God? Will you agree to keep his commandments, his testimonies and his statutes? Will you perform the words of the covenant in this book and love Yahweh with all your heart and with all your soul?"

The king paused and waited. For him, this was the centrepiece of his reign, his most important moment in a series of important moments of leadership. Would his

---

[74] Deuteronomy 29:10-15

people support him and make this commitment for themselves?

Isolated cries of "Yes!" began to break out through the crowd. Swiftly the responses spread, and calls echoed from all around: "We will!" shouted some, while others repeated, "Renew the covenant!" A man near me shouted, "We are the people of Yahweh!" and his friend standing next to him replied, "We will serve him!"

The king looked pleased, but repeated, "Will you perform the words of the covenant?"

"We will!" came the ecstatic shout of thousands of voices. Arms were waving, and some had stood and lifted their arms towards heaven in a gesture of acknowledgement of Yahweh, their God.

"If this is what you want," continued Josiah, "then all of you, stand[75] before Yahweh our God and repeat your commitment."

Those in the crowd who were not already standing rose to their feet[76], the young with all the ease and eagerness of youth, and the old with a solid determination to take the first steps towards a better direction in life.

"All that Yahweh has spoken we will do, and we will be obedient," said the king.

The crowd responded in unison: "All that Yahweh has spoken we will do, and we will be obedient!"

Everyone in the assembly looked at those around them, each seeing a sea of faces filled with a serious joy. There were many cheers and shouts, but many also seemed to recognise the importance of this moment, and maybe some saw the dangers ahead if the promise was not kept.

---

[75] 2 Chronicles 34:31-32

[76] 2 Kings 23:3

After a few minutes, the noise from the throng began to diminish and Josiah had the chance to continue; then we began to find out what "activities" he had been planning.

"Yahweh is a jealous God," he began. "He describes idols of wood and stone, silver and gold as 'detestable', but we have been worshipping such gods for generations. Over the last day or two as we have prepared Jerusalem to welcome all of you to the city in which God has put his name, I have seen many things with new eyes. I have realised that idolatry is everywhere in the city and all over the country. Even in my own palace, I have realised that there are altars of shame. Look towards my palace now," and Josiah pointed towards the very summit of the palace where an upper room stood by itself. On the side of the room, steps led up to the roof, and the wondering crowd saw on the roof a team of men surrounding two objects that were clearly altars[77]. "These altars have stood there throughout my life, and it is only now that I have realised that they must be destroyed, along with their pagan decorations. Yahweh, and only Yahweh, is our God. We must worship him only!"

The king raised his arm, which was obviously the signal for which the men on the roof had been waiting. Sledgehammers were raised and the team fell upon the first altar and demolished it. Another signal from the king followed and the second altar met the same fate. The sounds of iron on stone rang out clearly in the afternoon air, and most of those in the temple courtyard had a clear view of the destruction of the altars on the king's own roof.

"Idols must be destroyed and idolatry must be removed throughout the kingdom, even if it is found in

---

[77] 2 Kings 23:12

my palace or in the temple of Yahweh!" announced Josiah.

"What about these, my lord?"

The shout came from the gateway where I had finally recognised on that very morning, that the familiar horses and chariots were dedicated to the sun. A man stood next to one of the cast horses and patted it.

"What are they?" asked Josiah.

An officer of the temple, a man called Nathan Melech who supervised the gatekeepers, was standing near the gate and he shouted, "They are horses that earlier kings of Judah dedicated to the sun[78]."

"What are they made of?" called the king.

"I think they are made of bronze, my lord," answered Nathan Melech.

"Pull them down now and make sure that they are completely destroyed later," replied Josiah.

"These chariots aren't made of bronze," announced the man who had asked about the horses, "they're made of painted wood."

"Burn them then," responded the king. "Clear a space and burn them."

Some kindling was found to help start a fire, and the chariots were burnt to the sound of cheering. Sledgehammers and ropes were put to good use and the horses of the sun were soon lying amongst the flames as well.

This destruction of other people's symbols of idolatry was attractive to many in the crowd. It would become much harder once they returned home and looked around

---

[78] 2 Kings 23:11

their own houses and towns. But for the time being, the cleanup would continue.

"And what is this?" came another shout from across the courtyard, and an altar with various painted symbols on it was examined. The officers of the temple were called and the altar was pronounced to be one that had been built by Manasseh before his repentance[79]. Not only that, but the officers said that there was another in the other court of the temple. Two of Josiah's demolition gangs were called and both altars were quickly reduced to rubble, and the rubble was reduced to dust before being loaded into a cart for disposal.

All this time, Josiah still stood on the platform, making sure that the crowd was encouraged in this purification of the temple, but also keeping them under control. He now stepped forward again and issued a command to my father and the leading priests who managed the temple: "Any vessels, bowls, jugs, cups, or anything else that was made for Baal, Asherah, or any of the army of the sky, must be removed from the temple of Yahweh immediately[80]. I have many men here to help as necessary."

Meshullam, the Levite who had contributed so much in overcoming the plan to "modernise" the Book of the Law, called out to the king, "I can show your men where there is an Asherah pole[81]." He began to walk towards the back of the main temple building, followed by one of the king's demolition gangs.

Meanwhile, priests and Levites ran towards other parts of the temple and came back carrying bowls, jugs, spoons and many other items made of everything from wood to gold. They were all piled in a heap while carts

---

[79] 2 Kings 23:12
[80] 2 Kings 23:4
[81] 2 Kings 23:6

were brought in to take them away. Josiah's men kept a careful eye on the items to make sure that none of them went missing, particularly the ones made of gold or silver.

Shortly afterwards, Meshullam returned with the demolition squad who were dragging a large carved and painted wooden pole. An Asherah pole – hidden in the temple of Yahweh! The bright paint scraped off on the stone paving as the erstwhile object of worship was dragged unceremoniously across the court of the temple and loaded into a sturdy cart.

More and more items were being brought, items decorated with pictures of Baal and Asherah and all the starry host, but I had noticed that no-one was going near the building where that woman worked. Here was an opportunity to do something about it.

"What about that building there, my lord?" I called out to Josiah, trying to get his attention. There was quite a lot of noise around by this time, and it was not possible to make myself heard from where I stood. After a few tries, I started to push my way through the crowd until I was close to the wooden platform, looking up at Josiah.

"What about that building there, my lord?" I shouted, pointing to the building where I had seen the weaving and met that woman from whom I had fled. "That building is full of idolatrous objects and is used for horrible acts of pagan worship."

"Go and investigate," commanded Josiah, and a detachment of soldiers was directed towards the building. Examination showed that all the doors into the building were locked. One of the chiefs of the temple found a key for the door that I had entered through, but even with the key it could not be opened. Something was barring the way. And then came a delicious irony: at the suggestion of one of the soldiers, the condemned Asherah pole was taken off the cart and brought across to the door. Many soldiers lifted it up and used it as a battering ram – no doubt the best use it had ever been put to! The multitude cheered with each stroke as the heavy log thudded against the door. Loud shouts burst from many throats as the door was finally torn loose from its mountings. A symbol of idolatry had enabled us to break into this haven of idolatry.

Many soldiers entered the room and large quantities of embroidered and woven hangings were carried out and put into carts. Some were waved before the crowd to show their promotion of Asherah, but many were too disgusting for any public display. The fleeces and dyes, probably the ones that had been brought into the temple that very morning, were also taken out and loaded into carts for destruction. All the women in the rooms were taken into custody and led away for later trial, including that woman.

She did not look so confident now.

The doors to the other rooms were broken down also, and several men were brought out and led away to imprisonment and judgement. These were the sodomites whose activities Yahweh had revealed to me that morning. As the king began to realise the extent of the evil in this building, he made a quick decision. Several of the leaders of the army were near the wooden platform, and Josiah spoke to them. Immediately, one walked over to the building and issued commands. Flaming torches were brought and the hangings and fleeces were carried back into the building. Shortly afterwards, thin wisps of smoke began to curl through the doorways, slowly increasing until it billowed out of all doorways and other openings. Flames lit up the closer members of the crowd. The soldiers moved people back from around the building as the flames started to come through the roof, and within a short time, the roof fell in and flames and embers spurted out of the doorways. Fire would cleanse the building and destroy the items of worship and the beds of immorality, but Josiah had ordered that the building be completely destroyed and all its stones removed from the temple[82]. I was glad.

Much had already been achieved in removing idolatry from the temple of Yahweh, but the work that Josiah had planned for this day was not yet finished.

Many carts had been filled to overflowing with things that Josiah intended to destroy, and the soldiers now began to direct them out of the temple towards the gates of the city. The throng streamed out of the temple too, and some enthusiastic people made their way straight to the high places at the city gates. They would have liked to wreak havoc on the high places immediately, but agreed to wait for approval first; altars, idols and pagan symbols were all torn down[83] as soon as permission was granted.

The line of carts followed the road leading down into the Kidron valley[84]. Already, several large fires were burning in the valley near the brook – more of Josiah's preparations.

Down into the Kidron valley the crowd surged, surrounding the carts and cheering on the soldiers at their work. The vessels for Baal and Asherah and all the stars were thrown onto the fires, and the sparks and flames roared upwards. Those that could burn did so, and the heat distorted and defaced the rest. Never again would these vessels be used for the worship of gods who demanded the sacrifice of children and other horrific practices.

The Asherah pole was put on a fire of its own, and I rejoiced as its bright colours quickly faded and the eager

---

[82] 2 Kings 23:7
[83] 2 Kings 23:8
[84] 2 Kings 23:4, 6, 12

flames roved hungrily over the grotesque carved faces until they burst into flames of destruction.

Josiah followed the example of Moses' treatment of the golden calf in the wilderness as he commanded that the dust – all that was left of Manasseh's altars from the temple courts – be thrown into the brook Kidron[85]. The dust stained the water for some time, just as Manasseh's altars had sullied the worship of Judah for many years.

The king led many men across the brook Kidron and I went with them, eager to witness their work and hoping to get a little job of my own done too. On the other side of the brook Kidron, to the south of the Mount of Olives where King Solomon had built high places for his multitude of idolatrous wives, there was widespread destruction of these abominations, which had survived for 300 years, even through the reigns of righteous kings. Josiah had the courage and determination to desecrate and destroy them[86].

With joy, I was able to lead a few soldiers to the grove of trees opposite Anathoth and help them to demolish the shrine which was under construction there. Anathoth was a city of priests and should be dedicated to Yahweh. No longer would this shrine pollute the hillside.

$$\text{CR}$$

There was still plenty of work to do over the next few days. The Asherah pole burned slowly all night, and by the next morning it was reduced to dull grey ashes. Josiah ordered that the ash be beaten fine and then thrown onto the graves of the common people who had worshipped it[87].

---

85 2 Kings 23:12
86 2 Kings 23:13-14
87 2 Kings 23:6

The dust of the vessels taken from the temple and burned was also collected. Josiah had plans for it[88].

Each evening, darkness fell on a city made much cleaner by the destruction of many idols, altars, high places and other symbols of idolatry. During the hours of darkness, many more idols, carvings and paintings were hurled unmourned into the hungry fires in the valley of the Kidron.

The work continued for several days, in the temple and throughout the city. Joy of joys! – Topheth was desecrated, so that idolaters would not want to use it to sacrifice their children to Molech anymore[89], and large numbers of altars and idols were destroyed there also.

---

[88] 2 Kings 23:4
[89] 2 Kings 23:10

Chapter 15

Cleansing the land

Take care, lest you forget the covenant of the Lord your God, which he made with you, and make a carved image, the form of anything that the Lord your God has forbidden you. For the Lord your God is a consuming fire, a jealous God.

Deuteronomy 4:23-24

In a village south of Jerusalem, the morning after the reading of the Book of the Law dawned fine and clear. Late the previous night, by the light of a full moon, three men of the village had returned from Jerusalem where they had heard the words of God and renewed their covenant with him. Full of enthusiasm for the God of their fathers, they had arranged to meet together at dawn on the high place in the centre of their village.

When dawn came, inspired by the king's dedication, they tore down the Asherah pole and the altar to Baal, before starting work on the other altars arranged in a circle on the high place. Not many people were abroad in the quiet of early morning, but of the few who witnessed the attack, one was a priest. As a priest, he was not very particular about which god he served; he would represent any worshipper who asked him to present (and share in) their gift to any object that one might worship. Thus, when he saw the widening circle of destruction, he promptly roused the village, calling loudly for support.

Worshippers struggled from their beds and came to join the fray, but so did others who had also made the trek to Jerusalem the previous day. Explanations and discussions followed, and the idolaters learned that their king had approved of the destruction now being meted out to their idols and altars. Altars to idols like Baal, Asherah, Molech and Chemosh, or to any of God's created things, were all to be removed – with the king's support.

No-one dared to openly defy the king, so the enthusiastic trio actually gained some extra helpers and the work of destruction proceeded apace until the high place was cleared of idols and altars. Even the altar which had been used from time to time for the worship of Yahweh was torn down, with the acknowledgement that God wanted his people to worship him in his temple in Jerusalem.

I heard this story from one of the scribes who was copying the Book of the Law: his relative had been one of the enthusiastic trio, and he told me the story with glee. Other reports indicated that similar scenes had been enacted all over Judah, and thousands of idols and altars had been destroyed. Many carved and decorated pillars were torn down and used for firewood. As Josiah travelled around encouraging this purification, he even desecrated some of these places of false worship by spreading human bones around them[90].

Priests were a difficult problem throughout the country. Earlier kings had appointed many non-Levite priests, who had passed on their profession to their sons. These priests were normally dedicated to just one idol and Josiah forbade their work. Other priests, some of them even descendants of Aaron, had been content to work with any god that a worshipper asked for, including Yahweh. Still others, mostly a few descendants of Aaron, supported solely the worship of Yahweh, offering sacrifices and incense to him on local high places.

Josiah reformed the "industry". Only descendants of Aaron could work as priests or call themselves priests. Furthermore, worship was to be undertaken exclusively in Jerusalem. The high places scattered throughout the country in every town and village were to be destroyed – no-one was permitted to worship there. Descendants of Aaron who had served at the multitude of high places throughout the country were told to live in the cities of the Levites[91]. This was a major undertaking and property ownership in the cities of the Levites took several years to straighten out completely.

As demanded by the Book of the Law, Josiah commanded that the nation should worship Yahweh, and Yahweh alone.

These decrees took some months to clarify and promulgate, and the requirement that all men in the country should come to Jerusalem for the feast of the Passover went out with them. The Passover had not been kept since the days of King Hezekiah, more than 75 years

---

[90] 2 Kings 23:14

[91] 2 Kings 23:9 says that these priests did not go to Jerusalem, but that they ate food with their brothers.

before[92], but Josiah planned to keep the feast with all of its happy celebration of the blessings of God. In Jerusalem, the preparations began and continued throughout the winter.

Josiah, however, was not in Jerusalem at that time. Having travelled through many of the cities and towns of Judah supervising the destruction of high places and encouraging the residents to throw away their idols and worship Yahweh, he had set his sights further afield.

In the thirteenth year of his reign he had travelled into Israel and initiated some reform there also. Israel had long been a subject nation under the slowly decaying power of the Assyrian empire. Nevertheless, Josiah had been able to negotiate the opportunity to travel around the country almost completely unsupervised. Under the encouraging influence of King Josiah, the locals had destroyed or desecrated many idols and high places during that marvellous time.

Now Josiah wanted to repeat the visit. The discovery of the Book of the Law had brought an added urgency and clarified what God required of his people. The yearly cycle of feasts had been re-discovered and Josiah planned to invite the men of Israel to Jerusalem for the Passover, the first feast of the religious calendar. His enthusiasm carried his nobles and servants along with him, and he was sure that it would make a deep impression in Israel too.

Winter was fast approaching and Josiah wanted to visit Israel before the rains made travel uncomfortable and rendered some of the roads impassable.

Assyria's power was now waning rapidly and the empire was concentrating on its heart. Pressure was

---

[92] Hezekiah kept the Passover in 2 Chronicles 30:1-26 and there is no indication of any other Passover until the time of Josiah.

coming from the powerful nations to the south and east, and the remote provinces in the west warranted little attention. Nineveh was looking to itself. In fact, it was to be only ten years before Nineveh itself would be lying in ruins.

In this situation, Josiah approached the authorities in Israel from a position of some strength. The protective arm of Assyria had lost its power, and friendly negotiation had become an imperative in the provinces. Armed force could still threaten at times, but provincial administrations knew that it would be challenging to fulfil any such threats.

Josiah gave assurances that his motives were purely religious, and was welcomed with open arms. Religious and secular goals can be hard to separate at times, but it was certainly not Josiah's intention to extend his kingdom at that time[93].

The welcome was less grand than it had been five years before. The balance of power had shifted, and Josiah was now welcomed with greater respect despite his youth.

King Josiah had wanted to take my father with him, but he was unable to go because, although his ankle was much better, it still caused him a lot of pain at times: his visit to Jerusalem for the reading of the Book of the Law had left him unable to walk any significant distance for the last month. He had been unable to walk back to Anathoth that evening, and the visit of my mother's family had had to be rearranged. Instead of going to Anathoth, they had all stayed in the home provided for the High Priest in Jerusalem, and I had had little opportunity to spend much time with them as I had continued to deliver God's word at the temple gates to a newly attentive audience.

---

[93] Scripture does not tell us how Josiah was able to do what he did in Israel. However, there doesn't seem to have been any resistance.

Surprisingly, I was then invited to go to Israel with Josiah's party and accepted the invitation eagerly. Why had I been invited? I was too young to be a priest, taken along to teach or explain the law; I was deeply unpopular with some of Josiah's particular friends; and my prophecies criticised the kingdom and therefore, indirectly, the king. Not only that, but none of my prophecies had yet come true – as a prophet, I was completely untested. The only point in my favour was that my earlier words had fitted in with some of the words in the newly-discovered Book of the Law. However, as Azariah was fulfilling many of my father's duties in the temple and Gemariah did not want to leave home at the time because Hasshub had fallen seriously ill again, I suppose that I was the most available of all the men in my family.

☙

A large company set off with Josiah in the middle of the ninth month. The rainy season had begun in earnest, and significant amounts of rain were falling every second or third day. Fortunately there was no rain that day, and I remember the excitement and hopes that filled me as we set off towards Bethel, some walking and others in carts or on donkeys.

Travelling with a large group can be slow, particularly when there is the need to make arrangements for a large number of soldiers to enter a neighbouring country. It was the middle of the afternoon of the second day before we entered the gates of Bethel, and as I walked across the square inside the gate, I wished that I could visit Miriam and Maacah in their inn immediately. Of course, I didn't actually know if the inn would still be there, much less whether they would still be its proprietors. Much could have changed in the years since I had seen them last, but

I didn't want to think about that too much. They had been in the middle of a reformation in Bethel. Was the flame of reformation still alight in the town? The success or failure of Josiah's mission here might depend on the answer to that question. Dismissing, or trying to dismiss, the memories of a smiling face framed by long black hair, I followed the rest of the company to the building that was to house us for the next few days.

Josiah spent the rest of the afternoon in discussion with the local governor. Again, I learned that my business is not all the business in the world. Apparently, Josiah had kept in frequent and friendly contact with the northern kingdom ever since his visit five years before, and the governor had welcomed him as a friend.

Of course, I was not involved in the discussions, so I took the opportunity to go out into the streets of Bethel. Going straight to Miriam's inn, I was very pleased to find that she and Maacah were still there. Miriam looked to have put on a bit more weight and seemed to wheeze a little more as she moved around the inn. Maacah looked just as I remembered her, but with a little more maturity. Her lustrous black hair was still unobtrusively presented, but even more beautiful than I recalled. The voice I heard often in my dreams now sounded even more warm and welcoming, and her smile took my breath away. Should a prophet sent to the nations get married? The same sensible question came into my mind once more, but again, I pushed it away. For the time being, I had other questions that I wanted answers to, but I couldn't ask them directly.

"Tell me, what has happened in the inn, your lives and your faith since we last met?" I asked.

Miriam was the first to answer. "The inn has kept us busy, as you might expect. It's hard, though – the stairs keep getting steeper every year, and they surely wear a body out. Maacah's cooking is simply too good for my willpower!" She looked at me a little slyly and added, "When male guests sample the cooking and find out that Maacah is not married, they keep asking if they can marry her." Miriam had answered my unspoken question, and I felt that she probably knew she had done so.

Maacah looked embarrassed and changed the subject, unconsciously answering another of my questions. "Mother, Jeremiah will be more interested in the group of people we now meet with to share our worship of Yahweh. Since we have no temple here, our worship is probably a little different from yours in Jerusalem. Shobai found us some scrolls of scripture and we read them together on the Sabbath. We have no Levites or priests here, so we sing psalms, read some scriptures and discuss God's word together."

My heart leapt at this wonderful news. It thrilled me, but it didn't really surprise me – the faith of Miriam and Maacah had always seemed simple, but immovably sincere. Nevertheless, so many lose their way amid the multitude of idols that it was good to be reassured. I was fascinated to hear of their meeting together to worship and asked them more about what their worship entailed. Maacah explained that they knew tunes for many of the Psalms, so they could sing them or read them. They also had scrolls that told the history of the world from Adam onwards, including how Israel was led out of Egypt and the judges God had sent as leaders.

"You mentioned Shobai," I asked after a few minutes of discussion. "How is he? How often do you see him?"

"We see him on most Sabbaths – in fact, we saw him just two days ago. It is in his house that we meet together," replied Miriam. She looked a little sad, and I wondered why.

"*His* house?" I asked.

"Yes," answered Miriam, wrinkling her brow. "I'm trying to remember what happened when, and when you last visited us. The inn keeps me so busy that anything longer ago than yesterday might as well have been last year!"

"Jeremiah was last here more than two years ago, mother," replied Maacah.

"Yes," I agreed, "it was a little more than two years ago. That was the last time I saw any of you from Bethel."

"Ah, well, since then, Shobai has had a tough time, you know," Miriam mused. "A really tough time. A young woman, about your age or a little older, came to Bethel with her parents from a village near Shobai's farm. Shobai had already been speaking to her family about Yahweh as a living God and encouraging her parents to stop worshipping idols. The parents were not really interested, but the young woman, Eglah, was, and began to join us for worship. We had a beautiful opportunity to speak about Yahweh to someone who knew little about him, and then watch her faith in him grow. After a while, Shobai asked her parents if he could marry her, and they and Eglah agreed. Almost exactly a year ago, they were married, and it looked like the start of a wonderful life together. They were living in Shobai's parents' house, which I think you visited, but only two months later, Shobai's parents caught some sort of fever, and within just two days they were both dead. They were quite old, I suppose, and had lived full lives, but the suddenness of it left Shobai very upset. Once the inheritance was worked out with his older brother, Shobai ended up with his parents' house, so he and Eglah continued to live there. But the real tragedy came just two months ago. Eglah was expecting their first child, but it was a difficult birth and nothing could be done – she died in childbirth, and the child died also. Shobai was devastated. He has continued to do the normal things of life, but his heart still isn't in it." She finished with a sigh and looked at me sadly.

Tragedies happen all over the world every day, but life seems a bit too hard when such tragedies happen to people one knows without one even hearing about them. Over the years, God has told me about many future events, but most information I only find out when things happen, just like everybody else. In this case, I hadn't heard of it at all until two months later and I felt let down. While Shobai had been mourning the death of his young wife and his unborn child, I had been in Rabbah of the Ammonites in total ignorance of the tragedy. It seemed so sad, and I remember feeling that it wasn't very fair somehow. I had been away giving God's messages to uncaring foreign idolaters when I felt that I should have been supporting a faithful friend in his grief. It is easy to say that God knows best, and he does, but some events make it much easier to complain about God's ways.

"She was a lovely person," said Maacah, quietly, "and her faith was growing every day like a beautiful blooming flower. It was so encouraging to have a friend like her. She was not much older than me." Maacah looked sadly down at the floor for a few moments, and then looked up at me again. "You know how often Shobai used to smile?" she asked. "Eglah smiled almost as much. I miss her."

"Poor Shobai," I said. There wasn't much else that I could say.

Josiah's discussions that afternoon were very profitable. Not only did he renew his acquaintance with various leaders of the province of Israel and local leaders of Bethel, but he was also able to present his case for action against idolatry. And he presented it so convincingly that he was only waiting for a final confirmation from the leadership that his proposal for the removal of many altars, idols and high places could go ahead. This was expected to be a mere formality.

So how had he achieved this miracle? I wasn't involved in the discussions, but you couldn't look at the situation without believing that God must have had a hand in the outcome. Josiah had explained the current religious situation in Judah, including the discovery of the Book of the Law of Yahweh. He had described the improvements in the land following the removal of child sacrifice – an observable rise in the level of happiness across the nation in just the last two months. Not only that, but market stall holders and the leaders of cities and towns across Judah had been reporting remarkable reductions in thefts and violence. And all since the discovery of the Book of the Law.

Josiah had also mentioned two other main points to the leaders. The first was the existence of prophecies like mine which promised destruction, just as Jonah had promised for Nineveh. He pointed out that Nineveh had repented and was still a city more than 100 years later. The second was a reminder of how Yahweh had initially taught the people who had been brought to live in Israel by the Assyrians – using lions to kill those who did not worship him. Josiah managed to convince them that Yahweh had the power to punish and that he would do so, even if he didn't always do so straight away as he had when sending the lions. Punishment was coming, but repentance might still be able to turn it aside.

Confirmation of approval was expected in the morning.

ᚼ

That night in Bethel, clouds came with the evening and darkness fell swiftly. The temperature dropped too, and, shortly after dark, rain started. Heavy, driving rain fell all through the evening, and biting, icy showers continued through the night. When morning came with a dismal grey light fighting its way through the clouds, it was a damp and dreary day in Bethel. News came to us quite early that Josiah had been given approval to "take all necessary actions to enhance the worship of Yahweh in the city", but the rain throughout the morning prevented any such actions. It was cold, and we all stayed inside near a fire.

Miriam had mentioned that Shobai was expected in Bethel today – as long as he had finished helping his brother with the ploughing on their ancestral property. I was eager to see him, although I was not sure that I could help him in his present sorrow. As the rain continued to fall, I wondered whether he would arrive at all that day.

As we waited, I had an opportunity to talk with Ahikam, the son of Shaphan, and to get to know him a little better. We spoke about a wide range of subjects and he revealed a sharp and enquiring mind behind his urbane appearance. His major interest was civil administration, and he seemed to know a lot about it. He also had a strong interest in worship and the Book of the Law. As one of the representatives sent by Josiah to Huldah, he had heard God's message directly, and had been struck by the stringent requirements of Yahweh that were implicit in his response to Josiah. As seemed to be the case with almost everybody in Judah, he was surprised by Yahweh's demand that his people worship no other gods but him. When I used God's comparison of an unfaithful wife, he seemed to understand better, but he still wondered out loud how this could really work in daily life when other gods are everywhere. We spoke of the failed updates to the Book of the Law, my experiences in other countries, and many other things, as the rain fell steadily outside.

Shortly after noon, the weather began to improve and weak sunlight appeared through the clouds from time to time. After a little while, I braved the cold and made my way to Shobai's house, though with little hope that he would be there. It was with joy, therefore, mixed with a little trepidation, that I heard footsteps inside, and then the unlocking of the door.

"The Lord bless you, Shobai," I said as he opened the door.

"Jeremiah!" he replied and his familiar smile made an immediate appearance. "May Yahweh keep you. Come in." I stepped inside as Shobai asked, "What brings you to Bethel?"

"King Josiah has come to do what he can about the problem of idols, altars and high places here in Israel – and to invite everyone to keep the Passover in Jerusalem," I answered.

Shobai looked eagerly expectant all of a sudden and he laid a hand on my arm. "King Josiah? Here?"

"Yes," I replied, a little puzzled by his reaction.

"Come inside," he urged, "and I'll explain why this is so wonderful."

Shobai led me into an inner room and introduced me to a man who was waiting there. The reason why Shobai had braved the morning cold and trod the muddy road to Bethel in the rain this morning was that he had made an appointment to talk to this man. He was another farmer and worked a farm to the south of Bethel, between Bethel and the border with Judah. Shobai and he had met in Bethel about a month before when both had been selling produce, and Shobai had mentioned his thankfulness for the blessings of Yahweh in the abundant late figs he was selling. Some questions and an hour of discussion later, it was clear that this man was more interested in the worship of Yahweh than most, and enjoyed talking about the scriptures even though he knew little of them. Over the last month, Shobai had met with him several times and showed him some of the scrolls he had obtained over the last few years. Sadly, Shobai admitted that it had also helped to take his mind off his own troubles. At least that gave me an opportunity to show him a little of the sorrow and sympathy I felt.

This morning, Shobai had considered continuing their discussions to be more important than staying dry!

I need to explain a few things here. When I say that Shobai had several scrolls, you may get the impression that he was a rich man, but he wasn't. Rather, he was a determined and hard-working man who copied the scrolls that he wanted. Just as there had been in Judah, there were many "priests" in Bethel at that time, and although most were priests of the multitude of pagan idols worshipped in the city, a few were priests of Yahweh alone. Of course, most of these were not descendants of Aaron and should never have been appointed as priests at all; they were descendants of the people appointed by earlier kings of Israel who had wanted a job, and came from many different tribes. Most of these priests had some scrolls of religious texts, and the ones who worshipped Yahweh had various scrolls of Psalms, the law and the prophets. Some even had copies of the books of the chronicles of the kings, as they saw that many lessons could be learned from them. Over the last few years, Shobai had cultivated friendships with several of these priests and taken opportunities to copy some of their scrolls. The materials were still not cheap, but the main cost was the time taken in copying and Shobai gave that himself. His collection of scrolls represented an enormous personal commitment of time and effort.

We spent quite some time talking. Shobai explained why he was excited about the visit of Josiah, and that excited both his friend and me. From time to time, as we talked, we checked the weather, and found that it was improving slowly but steadily. After about two hours, I decided that it was time to return to Josiah's company before I missed out on any important action.

Shobai and his friend also decided to come along to watch. Shobai took with him one of his precious scrolls, carefully wrapped for protection against the weather.

಄

We were only just in time! As we walked up the road towards Josiah's lodgings, we saw a crowd in the street beginning to move up the hill away from us. Hurrying after them, we joined the crowd and soon found ourselves in an open area with a raised section in the middle which I recognised from an earlier visit. It was the high place at which Jeroboam the son of Nebat had corrupted Israel's worship with a golden calf so many years before. The Assyrians had taken the gold, but the high place and the altar remained. A carved Asherah pole also loomed large over the site of worship, which was unusually empty of worshippers. News had clearly been spread around that this was not a time for worship, but many had come to observe.

Josiah was gorgeously dressed in royal robes, and Shaphan stood with him to read some sections from the Book of the Law which condemned all worship of any god but Yahweh. Josiah's men, who had by this time had plenty of practice in the destruction of altars and high places, stood waiting and as soon as the announcements were finished, they carried out their task – breaking down the high place with all of its decorations and elegant stonework. The timber, including the Asherah pole, was piled up and burned, along with the flags and hangings bedecking the site. Jeroboam had built a massive altar, and now Josiah broke it down[94]. Many priests and wealthy worshippers had been buried near the high place and its altar – it was a coveted burial place. Josiah now took the bones from these special tombs and burned them on the ruined altar, defiling it in the eyes of its worshippers. One special tomb was visible near the altar, and Josiah called out to some of the bystanders, "What is this monument here?"

Full of excitement at seeing prophecy fulfilled before his eyes, Shobai called out, "O king, it is the tomb of the man of God from Judah who prophesied that a king called Josiah would do exactly what you are doing![95]" He held up a scroll and waved it before the crowd. "I have the prophecy written here in this scroll. Praise be to Yahweh, the only god who can foretell the future!"

"Praise Yahweh!" shouted a man nearby, and supporting shouts arose from all around. Those who had been doubtful about this desecration of such an ancient holy site were finally convinced, and many joined in this cleansing of God's land.

The bones of the prophet from Judah were left undisturbed, resting in peace, while the bones of those who had worshipped at the altar were consumed upon their broken altar[96].

---

94 2 Kings 23:15-16
95 2 Kings 23:17
96 2 Kings 23:16-18

Josiah had brought to Bethel the dust of the many vessels removed from the temple in Jerusalem and destroyed in the Kidron Valley. He scattered it, too, on the ruins of Jeroboam's altar[97].

Cℛ

Josiah obeyed the commands of Yahweh. High places, altars and idols were torn down and destroyed throughout Bethel and all the cities of Samaria[98].

Death came to the priests who had led so many astray[99] and the pure worship of Yahweh was given another chance. Men's bones fed the fires on the insatiable altars, before the altars too were destroyed and the fires flickered finally to extinction.

And as we travelled, the invitation was extended to all Israelites: When spring bursts out with new life, take hold of a new life of worship – come up to Jerusalem. Celebrate the Passover!

---

[97] 2 Kings 23:4 does not say what was done with the ashes. This is a guess.
[98] 2 Kings 23:19
[99] 2 Kings 23:20

Chapter 16

Joy and disappointment

March, 621 BC – the 18th year of King Josiah

Winter was over and the latter rains were easing. The first month of the religious calendar had begun and everyone was counting down to the end of the fourteenth day of the month when the Passover feast would begin[100].

My birthday came and went, and on the tenth of the month, families in all the areas close to Jerusalem chose a lamb to offer[101]. King Josiah had shown his wisdom and generosity by making arrangements to help those who were coming from further afield. People who were too far away to bring a lamb with them were to be assisted by the king, his nobles and the religious leaders – including my father. Those who were travelling greater distances would have to miss more of their work time and their travel would cost more, so it was only fair that they should have

---

[100] Exodus 12:5-6
[101] Exodus 12:3-4

some help with the greater costs. Of course, they would still be expected to bring some offerings, since God had said in the Book of the Law that no-one should appear before him empty handed[102]. They must also find somewhere in the city to stay – an impossible task unless extensive preparations were made to allow for the vast numbers of visitors that were expected in Jerusalem. Visitors from afar might add up to more than 500,000 people, and these would be in addition to the inhabitants of Jerusalem and the towns nearby. Overall, Jerusalem would need to fit between about 700,000 and 800,000 people for the week of Passover, and this was the reason why preparations had begun even before winter had arrived.

Special arrangements were made whereby Jerusalem could welcome many more visitors than would normally be possible. Josiah had decided to have dwellings constructed where widows and orphans would be able to stay with no expenses for food or board. The inhabitants of Jerusalem were encouraged to open their houses to extras – relatives if they had them, or any strangers from far away who needed a place to stay. However, they were warned that any charging of exorbitant fees would attract the attention of the king, and he would not look on it with a kindly eye.

Provision had been made for storing extra water in the city, and non-perishable foods were being stored in nearby towns ready for immediate delivery as the feast progressed.

The temple was being cleared of everything that was not essential. Open space would be vital to allow the masses of worshippers to visit God's holy house, and

---

[102] Deuteronomy 16:16

awnings were placed wherever possible to keep everyone dry should the latter rains recommence.

Preparations were being made everywhere, and many helpers had been brought into Jerusalem from outside. Already, the city was teeming with people, and more came every day.

And still the main body of worshippers was not due until the fourteenth day of the month – another three days.

My father's ankle was much improved, although he still walked with a slight limp that would never leave him. He and two other officers of the temple had agreed to give 2,600 lambs[103] for those who had none. This would provide enough meat to feed about 25,000 to 40,000 people[104], but what was that when so many were expected to come? Until then, I hadn't really understood quite how rich my father was. Kish, the father of Saul, the first king of Israel, was described as a man of wealth, yet he had sent his son to find just a few asses[105]. My father was able to give almost a thousand lambs and still have many more remaining. I was very pleased to see some of the riches being used to help others in worship. It seemed appropriate for the High Priest to use his wealth this way. While I still had questions about my father's wealth, at least now it was being used for God, however it had been obtained[106].

My father's efforts to bring me back into the mainstream of Levite activity had begun again, and this time they were harder to resist. Although I was not yet old enough to work as a priest, I was now twenty-two, and

---

[103] 2 Chronicles 35:8

[104] Assuming each lamb or goat would have enough meat to feed 10-15 people, based on Exodus 12:4.

[105] 1 Samuel 9:1-3

[106] Deuteronomy 23:18 would still have to be considered

King David had commanded that Levites over the age of twenty were to be included in the work of the temple[107]. What should I do? The work of prophesying had kept me busy for the last few years, but at the moment, God had given me no specific work of prophecy to do.

I was ritually clean; I knew the commands about the Passover thoroughly from my reading of many scrolls; and it was clearly my duty to serve in the temple, if no specific commands from Yahweh overrode it. So I joined the thousands of Levites who were being thoroughly instructed in what was required[108] as they trickled into Jerusalem from the many towns of the Levites.

Josiah had been determined to read and understand the Book of the Law of Yahweh, but he had also continued on to study other scrolls of scripture. He had read the records of the regulations of David and Solomon with regard to the operation of the temple, and from them he had gained at least as much understanding of how the temple should be used as any of the priests, and more than most. As the time for the Passover approached, Josiah gave orders regarding the preparations for the Passover: instructions for the organisation of the Levites and priests by their ancient family groupings, and following the rules as to who did what. In the wilderness, priests had carried the ark of the covenant on their shoulders whenever the tabernacle moved[109], and this had continued until it was placed in the temple built by Solomon[110]. But at some point in history, and nobody knew quite when, the ark of

---

[107] 1 Chronicles 23:24-27

[108] 1 Chronicles 23:28-32

[109] Deuteronomy 31:9, 25; Joshua 3:3; 2 Samuel 15:25, 29. Numbers 4:15-16 may suggest that the Kohathites carried the ark initially in the wilderness, but if so, this was only temporary, probably while there were too few priests.

[110] 2 Chronicles 5:7

the covenant had been taken out of the temple. Maybe it had been removed for safekeeping during the rule of Manasseh, or possibly even earlier in history. Our records have no definitive mention of the ark being in the temple after the time of Solomon.

King Josiah now ordered that it be reinstated in the temple. There was, he said, no reason why it should be carried around by the priests when the temple had been designed and built to contain it[111].

Josiah and his leaders, including the chief men of Jerusalem and the leading priests, had made plans for everything. Nothing must be allowed to go wrong. Never before in the lifetime of any of those attending had this kind of event occurred, so everything needed to be thought through and planned in minute detail. Capable men were appointed to oversee all of the arrangements: men in charge of collecting, protecting and feeding thousands of lambs on the hills near Jerusalem; men in charge of assigning people to accommodation; men to welcome visitors, explain the main events, and answer any questions the visitors might have; men to arrange water supplies; men to arrange for extra food supplies to be available, particularly since all bread must be unleavened for the duration of the feast; men in charge of rubbish removal, since the massive influx of visitors would overwhelm the ordinary handling of rubbish; men and women to prepare and distribute food amongst the orphans and widows.

Each of these areas of work had many others working under the direction of these leading men. Thousands were involved in the effort to make the Passover a celebration for all.

---

[111] 2 Chronicles 35:3

The organisation of events and people within the temple was a matter organised separately by the leading priests and Levites. If you try to think of all the matters that need arranging for a Passover, you will begin to understand how much work there was to keep everyone busy. Both priests and Levites must be ritually clean to work in the temple, yet few people actually knew in detail what this meant. Those who did, passed on their knowledge to others in large classes held in the temple.

Many people were expected to bring gifts and offerings to the feast, making vows and commitments to the service of Yahweh. Levites and priests needed to know what gifts were acceptable, which dedicated gifts must be valued by them, and how such a valuation should be done. These were all matters that should be covered in the education of priests and Levites before they are old enough to begin their work, but much of this fundamental background had been lost.

Strenuous work over the winter had helped to sort out some of the documentary evidence for our religion. Many scrolls that were clearly flawed, falsified copies had been destroyed, while older, more accurate scrolls were treated with respect again, even if their contents weren't always appreciated by the more modern, liberal scribes. I had been very pleased to be able to be involved in some of this work, and my background of reading God's word almost every day for the past five years had been of great value. The large cache of scrolls in our scroll room had been a tremendous boon too, and I had begun to feel more confident in distinguishing between the genuine works of scripture and the false and misleading works of dishonest, sycophantic or evil scribes.

Many things had to be arranged in the temple for the worshipping populace: teaching sessions where visitors and locals could be instructed in the law of Yahweh; guides to lead worshippers to the right places in the temple for their worship; men to kill the many thousands of lambs; men to dispose of the blood of the lambs; men to lead choirs in praise of Yahweh; men to clean up the temple area continually; and men who were just to be available to do anything that might be needed at any time.

CR

Eager visitors were already arriving by the twelfth day of the month. Those who had relatives in the city needed no help finding a place to stay, but others took advantage of the accommodation organised within Jerusalem. Men, women and children had all braved the early spring weather with the possibility of cold and rain and were excitedly waiting for the celebrations to begin.

I was waiting impatiently for Shobai to arrive from Bethel, and hoping that Miriam and Maacah would be able to come with him, and possibly others as well. When I had left Bethel in early winter, Miriam had been very eager to come, but not certain that it would be possible because of the inn. I was fairly sure that when she considered the importance of this feast, she would come whether it was convenient or not, but I had not heard any news since then.

Shobai had expected to arrive late in the afternoon of the thirteenth day of Nisan, and as the morning passed I was surprised at just how excited I felt. Everything in Jerusalem was building up to a climax, and everyone seemed to be excited and a little nervous.

That morning saw the completion of our training for the work of the Passover, and I then spent the afternoon at the Benjamin Gate watching the visitors arrive. Happiness was the overriding expression on people's faces as they approached the gate, and joyful sounds filled the air. Merchants were still plying their trade by the sides of the road, but even they seemed to share the communal good mood. Josiah had forbidden them to sell lambs[112], but they had many other sorts of things to sell to the visiting crowds, and were having enough success to keep them happy.

As I watched, seated in a raised place where I could see out of the gate over the heads of the crowd, thousands of people entered in a steady stream. Some of them had obviously made the longer journey from Israel, but locals were coming too. I saw my childhood friends Adaiah, Chelub and Benaiah in the crowd together, although the latter two tried to avoid my eye – which was made difficult by Adaiah when he saw me and came across to greet me! Adaiah at least had come to the reading of the Book of the Law, which had pleased me. Maybe the other two had now recognised their error and were trying to turn back to God. I hoped so. All of the visitors were greeted by the men who had been appointed to welcome visitors and explain what would be happening and what help was available in arranging accommodation for visitors.

A number of the visitors from the north looked vaguely familiar, and I concluded that I must have seen them when I had travelled into Israel with Josiah just a few months before. A few even looked at me with faint recognition, so presumably they remembered me. I had presented God's words to Israel in quite a few places as we had travelled around, and some people had obviously noticed. Once again I was reminded of the heavy responsibility that goes with being a prophet to the nations. After people hear God's word from me, they notice how I behave the next time they meet me. How easy it would be for me to let God down and give them an excuse to ignore God's message!

---

[112] There is no evidence for this, but since the king and his nobles were providing so many lambs, I am assuming that there would have been no need for anyone to pay for lambs.

As I was contemplating this, I saw more familiar faces in the approaching crowd. It sounds silly, but I think my heart stopped for a while when I saw Maacah, and I quickly jumped down from my vantage point and ran out to meet Shobai and the others with him. Running to meet friends did not seem the grave and dignified behaviour that might be expected from a prophet with a very serious message to convey to a nation under threat of destruction, but all I can say is that a sudden smile had taken away all thought of being a prophet to the nations. Maacah had seen me over the crowd also, and as our eyes met, her smile had filled me with joy. Even now, looking back over the years, I still feel a little sad about what happened during that week.

We met some distance from the gate. Shobai was leading, and he too smiled as he saw me. It was balm to my soul to have friends who were genuinely pleased to see me.

Miriam was breathing heavily, and greeted me with a bit of a wheeze, saying, "The hills around here are almost as steep as the stairs in the inn, but it's worth coming! What a beautiful sight it is when Jerusalem and the temple first come into view! You people in Judah obviously love the temple and look after it carefully."

She stopped to take a few gulps of air, and Shobai agreed, looking at me a little doubtfully. "Jeremiah, I thought you said that the temple wasn't in very good condition."

"It wasn't," I confirmed, "but the last few months have made all the difference."

I then turned to greet the other two couples from the small dedicated group of believers in Bethel whom I had already met when I was there, and Shobai introduced me to another couple who had joined them since that time. Nine people who met together on Sabbaths when they could, to talk about Yahweh and his ways. And now their horizon would be expanded by attending the temple in Jerusalem for the feasts and sharing worship with many more people.

I felt rather awkward greeting Maacah, but it was what I had been waiting for all day, and seeing her had been worth the wait.

We entered the city together, then Miriam and Maacah were led off to the accommodation set aside for widows and orphans. It suddenly occurred to me that I didn't know very much at all about Miriam's husband and how she came to be a widow.

The afternoon was declining, and it was best to make sure that everyone knew where they would be resting their head that night. Shobai and the others came with me to the accommodation allocation centre and I led them to one of the helpers whom I had already spoken to about this group, although at that time I hadn't known exactly how many would be arriving. Visitors from Israel were particularly welcome, although they had to answer various questions about their parentage and whether the men were circumcised – to make sure that they truly were Israelites and not Gentiles.

Already the city was crowded. No streets were empty and all homes had many people within. About 350,000 extra people had already been squeezed into the city and the rest could be expected to arrive in crowds throughout the next day. All over the city, tents had been erected in open spaces, fastened to houses or even set up on the roofs of houses. The roadways were narrowed by hastily erected enclosures where people could overflow from houses to sleep outside in the crisp spring air. Though it was the time for the latter rains, there had been no rain in the last two days. Would the dry spell continue? No-one knew, and no-one knew whether to pray for it to continue or not. Rain meant growth and food for all later in the year, but rain at this time meant inconvenience and distraction from the worship all had come to offer to the God of Israel.

Shobai and the others were led to the house of a well-off but generous young couple who had agreed to accommodate visitors, and I followed. The couple welcomed the group and introduced themselves as Zaccai and Abigail saying that they were particularly pleased to have visitors from Israel staying in their home. Their hearts had been touched by the laws of Yahweh which they had heard in the temple when King Josiah had read the Book of the Law. When the king had asked for people to welcome visitors for the Passover, they had offered their house. They were from the tribe of Judah and were actually quite close relatives of King Josiah. Zaccai worked for the king as a junior advisor and was probably only a year or two older than I, while Abigail his wife looked to be about the same age as Maacah. They had no children yet, but were rich enough to own a large house which could welcome these visitors with no difficulty. In fact, it was their plan to take in more visitors if they found that things worked alright with these seven.

Zaccai and Abigail welcomed us warmly, and within a very short time an animated discussion was ranging to and fro across the long history of the Passover, our nation and the wonders of Yahweh's love. Zaccai was clearly surprised and impressed by Shobai's knowledge of our scriptures. The people of the northern kingdom were widely criticised in Judah for their ignorance of Yahweh and their paganism, but Shobai had taught himself from the word of God, piece by piece, over the last six or seven years.

By the end of these discussions, I was convinced that Shobai was a little different from when we had met on previous occasions. But though his ready smile was less common – testament to his sorrow at the sudden death of his wife – there was no difference in his strong attachment to God.

We had arranged to meet Miriam and Maacah and proceed with them to the High Priest's house where my parents were staying for the feast, and the time was fast approaching. When Zaccai and Abigail heard of our plans, they asked if it would be more convenient for Miriam and Maacah to move to their home. A small room at the back of the house was free for them as long as they would be content with that. I immediately went to ask them if they would appreciate this change, and they gratefully repacked their belongings and returned with me to the house. The beds in their original accommodation would be sure to be used by others as the city continued to fill.

Back at Zaccai's house, Miriam and Maacah were quickly established in the small room at the back.

Our next stop was the High Priest's house. My mother had been eager to meet Shobai and his friends after my glowing references to them. Later I suspected that she had gathered a little more from my praise than I had meant her to see, and specifically wanted to meet this girl whom I had only mentioned in passing as "a good singer". In blissful ignorance of this, we entered the house and I introduced all of the visitors to my mother. As usual, our conversation moved directly into a discussion about God, as conversations were wont to do when Shobai was involved – or my mother, for that matter. When the Psalms were mentioned, my mother said to Maacah, "Jeremiah said that you sing the Psalms very nicely."

It was true, but I wished that my mother hadn't mentioned it.

The next morning dawned in a blaze of beautiful sunshine with not a cloud in the sky, and I felt just the same myself. I had never felt happier in my life and there was not a cloud on my horizon. My nation was turning to God in a way that had not happened for hundreds of years: Huldah's words had worked as Jonah's had. And the young woman who increasingly filled my thoughts was here in Jerusalem and had been pleased to see me. My mother had also seemed pleased with her, and that would be important.

As soon as the sun lit the sky, the trickle of people who had continued to arrive overnight, grew again to a torrent as crowds poured into Jerusalem. A look over the walls or through the gates showed throngs approaching from all directions. Every hour, thousands came in through each gate of the city, and Josiah's exhaustive arrangements were tested to the limit. There was no more space inside the city, and newcomers were being accommodated outside the walls in neat lines of tents. Special cooking areas were set up as had been planned beforehand, and helpers were on hand to provide advice and answer any questions about what was needed for the Passover. And still the crowds kept coming. Noon passed as the thousands of lambs provided by the king, his nobles and the leading priests were brought into the gate area near the temple. The noise was incredible. I took my place and made sure that I was washed and ready for the coming onslaught.

King Josiah's men who had wisdom with numbers had discussed with the leading priests the massive job of killing all of the necessary lambs, and an early start had been agreed upon. With about 40,000 lambs to be offered, allowing four hours would still require 10,000 offerings per hour. Even disposing of the blood had required significant planning.

What an experience it was! People arranged themselves in groups of 10-15 and two representatives of each group went to the gate of the temple. Locals took their lambs with them, while visitors from further away were provided with lambs by the gatekeepers – a generous gift indeed. The men then moved into the temple area and waited, while the voices of the choir of the descendants of Asaph – appointed to this work hundreds of years before by king David – filled their ears. Psalms came to life through their voices and, with the added beauty of the musical accompaniment, they moved many of the worshippers to tears. The next available Levite killed the lamb and drained the blood into a basin. As soon as possible, a priest took the blood and sprinkled it in the temple.

After the sprinkling of the blood, more Levites were waiting to skin the lamb before returning the carcass to the waiting men, who carried it back to their companions to be roasted whole.

Tens of thousands of lambs fed hundreds of thousands of men, women and children in Passover celebrations that night.

Darkness fell over a city ringed with countless fires, while the fires of a multitude of burnt offerings also lit the temple within. Scattered through the length and breadth of the city, more fires roared furiously, roasting flesh. The age-old walls lay strong and secure under the gleam of a full moon shining from a cold, clear sky. Sounds of joy and happiness filled the air and echoed around the hills. The scene was a beautiful, timeless celebration of the love and power of Yahweh, the one who brought our people out of Egypt.

The eye of God was upon his people.

As good as it gets? Yes, this was the peak, the pinnacle of the greatness of King Josiah. This truly was as good as it got.

Thirty-five years later, I would again see Jerusalem ringed with fires and watch in horror as fire consumed the city – even the temple itself. Those fires also would roast much flesh.

❧

The Passover that year was such a happy time, and the Feast of Unleavened Bread continued in its wake with my joy growing every day. I had more opportunities to see Maacah than I had ever had before, and my hopes and plans began to grow. Once again, I pushed aside my doubts about the wisdom of a prophet marrying, and determined to speak to my father as soon as the feast was over.

There were just two days of the feast remaining when, as I was preparing to pray early in the morning, I felt the familiar kindling of a fire within me. Light within, and a heat unbearable. A presence, so pure and white. A feeling of purpose that far outshone all my hopes and aspirations, a purpose which comforted, yet took away my hopes of happiness in a single stroke. The voice of Yahweh said to me:

"You shall not take a wife,
nor shall you have sons or daughters in this place."[113]

Maacah could never be my wife.

---

[113] Jeremiah 16:2

Free Download

Paul in Snippets

A 109-page PDF novelette by Mark Morgan.

The life of Paul painted from the Acts of the Apostles.

Get your free copy of *Paul in Snippets* when you sign up for the Bible Tales mailing list. As well as the eBook, you will receive a weekly email newsletter with micro tales, informative articles and special offers.

Visit **http://www.BibleTales.online/free-pins**

www.BibleTales.online

Bible Tales Online

Other books by Mark Morgan are available from Bible Tales Online including other books in this series.

Terror on Every Side!

The Life of Jeremiah

From a family of priests in the peaceful reign of good King Josiah, came a young man Jeremiah, bringing words from God to his people. It was no message for the fainthearted, either. It was a message of *Terror on Every Side!*

Volume 1 – Early Days
Volume 2 – As Good As It Gets
Volume 3 – Darkness Falling
Volume 4 – The Darkness Deepens
Volume 5 – No Remedy

Generally available as paperback, eBook and audiobook.

To find the list of currently available books, visit

http://www.BibleTales.online/books